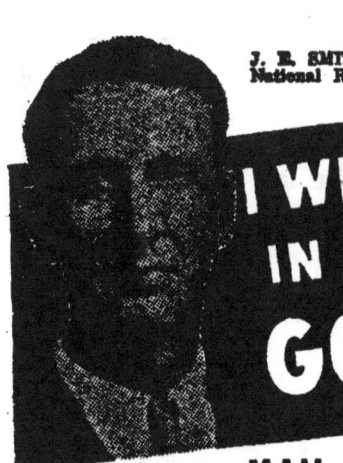

When answering advertisements please mention SPICY-ADVENTURE STORIES

1

SPICY-ADVENTURE STORIES

June, 1936   Vol. 4, No. 3

CONTENTS

SPICY-ADVENTURE STORIES is published by the Culture Publications, Inc., 900 Market St., Wilmington, Del. The Publisher assumes no responsibility for the return of unsolicited manuscripts.

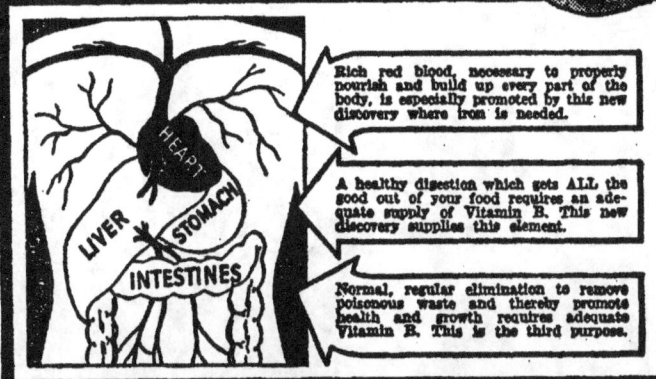

HUMP OF

By
JOSE
VACA

He's a lone wolf, the Sabinas Kid, whether he's after a vicious dope ring or a single lovely girl

JOE POBLANO, the fat cook of the Hong Kong Cafe, eyed the dishwasher with a worried gleam in his deepset eyes. That fellow looked like no dishwasher Joe had ever seen! He leaned over the steaming sink, arms immersed to the elbows in the suds, a dirty apron wrapped twice about his slim waist. Juan Pistolas, he called himself! As if an honest man could have a name like that! Fat Joe regarded the hawk-like profile from the corner of his eye,

SERRANO

At the crack of the pistol Serrano leaped
backward as if struck by a giant hand.

stirred the stew of *cabrito* simmering on
the huge gas stove and wondered where
he had seen the man before.

The door to the kitchen burst open
and Helen Freeman trotted in. Blonde
and vivacious, as rounded in spots as she
was depressed in others, Helen was a
favorite around Papa Nick's Hong

Kong Cafe. She reached down to tug
at long silken hose, to raise a dress hem
carelessly, exposing a two inch strip of
gleaming white flesh above her stocking
tops. As she leaned, the lowcut neck of
her trim uniform revealed a hint of the
deep, dusky valley between prominent
breasts.

Joe Poblano drew in his breath quickly, expelled it in a hissing explosion that threatened to rupture his immense stomach. His little eyes were popping from his head. Helen looked up quickly, made a moué with red lips.

"Okay, snap out of it, *amigo!* I've got an order of *tacos* and *enchiladas* coming with *chili con queso* on the side and be damn' sure the *tortillas* are crisp!" She saw Juan Pistolas, the dishwasher, walked toward him with a gallant swing to her stride.

"Hello, handsome, finding any pearls?"

White teeth flashed in a brown face. Juan Pistolas said, "No pearls but one, *senorita.* You are the only pearl I find in this place of sweat and hard work!"

She grinned, laid a hand caressingly on his shoulder, probed with red fingertips at the rippling muscles beneath the flesh. Her smile was a challenge. A stool stood near by. She kicked it closer, crawled atop it and crossed her legs in a great wave of billowing uniform, sheer chiffon, and gleaming flesh. "When are you coming to see me, Juan?" Her voice was low, caressing, daring. "I get awfully lonesome!"

JUAN PISTOLAS turned from his sink, swept her provocative figure with bold eyes, from slim ankles past rounded calves, flattened thighs, bold pointed breasts and rouged face. She flushed, thrilled inwardly, half stretched out a hand.

"Me, *senorita*, Juan Pistolas," his voice was low, "I am but a dishwasher."

"Don't let that worry you," she breathed, "I'm only a waitress. There's a good show at the Grande tonight. I'll pay the way and afterward—" Her arched brows, her dancing eyes, were a promise.

"Helen! For the love of God wait on your customers!" Papa Nick, the cafe owner, almost as fat as Joe Poblano ambled through the door. His fat hand closed on her arm in a possessive gesture, pulled her from the stool. "Do I pay you to stand around with the cheap help when guests are in the house? Tomas Serrano is in the front and wants you. Go quickly."

The girl made a face of disgust, slapped his hands aside and said, "That damn' hunchback! He gives me the creeps!"

At the sink Juan Pistolas clattered the dishes. But he had heard the words of Papa Nick. As the door swung to, he wiped his hands on his apron, headed toward the cafe.

"*A donde va?*" snapped Poblano waspishly.

"To pick up the dirty dishes," smiled Pistolas and was gone. Unobstrusively he walked down the aisle back of the counter nearly to the front where a great tin tub of dirty dishes awaited. He leaned over as if to pick them up but his black eyes were narrowed, fixed on the occupants of the booth opposite.

Tomas Serrano, the *jorobado*, the hunchback, sat in all his gaudy finery, a multi-colored *serape* about his crooked shoulders, a broad white sombrero pushed back from his high forehead. Across from him Jim Taylor, the American ranchman, drunk as usual. Papa Nick stood before the booth beside Helen who was trying to get an order from the men.

Serrano's yellow fingers were on her shoulder, seemed to be probing, caressing. The girl flushed, tried to pull away.; the fingers bit deeper. She half cried out in pain while the men roared with laughter.

JUAN PISTOLAS seized a dirty silver knife, drew back his hand. It swished through the air in a gleaming arc while Pistolas stooped, dropped to his knees and scuttled away on all fours. Tomas Serrano let out a shrill scream of pain and anger, regarded the blood on the back of his hand with savage amazement. As if by magic a pistol leaped from his armpit. Humped over like a great spider he whirled into the next booth, ready to avenge his insult.

Back near the kitchen door Juan Pistolas raised up, a tub of dirty dishes in his hands, whistling faintly. Papa Nick, Taylor, and Serrano glared in his direction but dismissed a humble dishwasher as an assailant!

In the kitchen Joe Poblano's eye was more fishy than ever. He had seen it all through the glass in the door. This man was no dishwasher! He started to say something but Pistolas put the tub of dishes on the rack, turned to the fat cook with his hands resting lightly on his hips, his body bending forward from the slim waist.

"Well, *amigo?*" he said and smiled. The smile wasn't pleasant to look at; it was too much like that of a wolf.

Poblano sputtered, "Well, nothing, to be sure, nothing! That Serrano is a bad one for sure!"

"Who is Serrano, Joe?"

"Serrano? Why he is the owner of the huge hacienda on the road to La Gloria across the Mexican line. He comes here once a week to get drunk and see his friends. In a little while he will go upstairs to a private room and there will be many come to see him. *Senoritas* and *caballeros* and doctors and big men of this town. Serrano, he knows them all!"

JUAN PISTOLAS was deep in the greasy dishwater when Helen came in again to give the order. She eyed

him with sudden wonder for she had seen the flash of the arm, the gleam of the knife as he ducked low behind the counter. In a low voice she said, "Thanks," pressed close to him so that he thrilled to the warmth of her soft body. Before she could say more, Papa Nick bustled in.

"Serve Serrano in the private room upstairs, Helen, and," he caught her shoulder, wheeled her around, "please to remember he is a man with very much money. You are to amuse him."

She bowed her head with a hopeless look, left the kitchen.

At exactly six o'clock Juan Pistolas hung his dirty apron on a hook and climbed into a blue jumper. A disreputable black hat was set carelessly on his tousled head. "You aren't going to eat?" questioned Joe Poblano, patting his fat pouch.

"Tonight I am very busy," answered Juan. "Business always before the pleasure." He paused to look through the glass section of the swinging door into the cafe and then turned and hurried out the back door.

Around the first garbage can he dropped suddenly to his knees, peered back at the kitchen to see if he was watched. Joe Poblano was eating. He would see and hear nothing!

A small shed leaned against the back of the restaurant building. With the agility and noiselessness of a cat Juan Pistolas scaled its tottering walls. His feet made no sound on the tin-covered roof.

An open window let him into the upper floor of the Hong Kong Cafe. For a moment he stood silently listening. From one of the private rooms down the hallway he heard the drone of conversation, a thin crack of light showed beneath the closed door. For a long moment he listened at the top of the stairway, heard the clatter of dishes, the rattle of silver coming from below. Then he went back to the closed door, stooped, applied an eye to the keyhole.

"The dog!" he snarled to himself. Tomas Serrano, the hunchback, and Papa Nick, the cafe owner, were not alone in that room. In fact they were invisible. The only man in Juan's line of vision was Dr. Howard Murray, the most respected and most sought after doctor in the whole city. Even as Pistolas watched, he saw the doctor lay a great stack of bills on the table before him, saw a lean, clawlike hand whose back was crisscrossed with white tape come into the scene and pick up the money. In a few seconds a black box some three inches square made its appearance on the table. Dr. Murray picked it up, dropped it carelessly into his open kit which sat beside him on the floor.

There came the sound of slow footsteps ascending the stairs. Hurriedly Pistolas opened the door of the next room, dove inside, leaving the door open a tiny crack. Before the newcomer appeared, Dr. Murray emerged, hurried down the hall, spoke briefly to the ascending party and hurried on. Juan Pistolas gasped as the newcomer came into the dimly lighted hallway.

It was Helen Freeman and her face looked as if she were going to her death. She was in street clothes, a sheathlike dress that clung lovingly to a rounded, supple figure, swaying breasts and tapering thighs. For a moment she paused. Papa Nick stuck his leonine head out the door and called. On lagging feet she came.

JUAN PISTOLAS was fumbling in the pocket of the jumper. As she entered the door he sprang forward soundlessly, a three inch strip of stiff cellophane in his hand. Neither the girl nor Nick saw the shadowy figure. Nick swung the door closed. Juan Pistolas slipped the stiff cellophane across the lock. The door slammed shut. But the lock failed to slide into the groove made for it. The cellophane held it out. Again Pistolas crouched at the keyhole.

He held his breath for Tomas Serrano had walked into the view to seize the girl by the front of her dress. The girl cowered back. A look of evil glee appeared in the cruel eyes of the Mexican.

"So," he said softly sibillantly, "just as I have suspect you are a stool pigeon. Today I find it all out, my dear. You have been put here by that damned American gangster, Maroni, to find out what you can. Very well, you shall tell me what you have found out."

"No, no," said the girl. "I'm not what you think. I'm—" She tried to pull away. The talon-like hand pulled her closer. A hard palm reached up to slap her viciously on the cheek. The dress gave with a ripping sound. Breasts, suddenly half freed, vibrated, in the glaring light. She covered them with her palms.

"You won't scream," sneered the Mexican, gloating at the sight of the white flesh. "You're a crook yourself. Now will you tell me or—" *Whop!* A quirt in his right hand slapped suddenly, ominously, across the table. The girl cowered still farther away. Nick shoved her back with an oath. The fingers of Tomas Serrano, the repulsive hunchback, clawed at her clothing, ripping it to tatters, tore the dress from her white body. Clad only in scanty brassiere, brief step-ins and chiffon hosiery she stood there cowering, her lips a thin quivering line of red in her white face.

This man was no dishwasher; any one could sense it.

"Again," roared Tomas, "I ask you, what do you know of us?"

"Nothing," she moaned, "I'm not—"

The quirt descended across her bare shoulders, left a raw red wake across tender skin, the tasseled ends cutting deep into the flesh of one soft breast, crossing the tender skin with cruel bruises. She moaned. Tomas Serrano raised the lash again.

PISTOLAS opened the door, stood there framed by the darkness. He said, "Hello, *amigos.*"

Nick gasped. "Get out," he managed to grate but the only answer he got was a white-toothed snarl. Serrano dropped the whip, stood in a half crouch, his burning little eyes fixed on the face of the newcomer.

"Go right ahead," grinned Pistolas. "I, too, would like to know what the lady knows."

"You! *You*—" said the hunchback, his eyes suddenly wide with fear. "Now I know you. Listen, we will take you in with us. You shall have half, my friend. You—"

"Stop!" Pistolas' voice was cold, commanding. "I know you, Serrano, also, and I know your game. I want no part of it. You recognize me, Serrano?"

Little by little Papa Nick was edging toward the door. The girl stood where she was, shielding her nakedness with the palms of her hands, her eyes wide and fixed on the newcomer.

"*Si!* I know who you are," whispered Serrano, the hunchback. His pockmarked face was yellow with fear. Great beads of perspiration stood on his brow, only the whites of his eyes were visible. Nick's fat hand was on the door.

Suddenly, without taking his eyes from the man before him, Juan Pistolas lashed out backward with a heel. It caught Papa Nick squarely in the groin, caused him to double up in nausea, and slide slowly to the floor. From the corner of his eye Juan watched him, said, "Sit there, great pig. I have business with you later. And you, Serrano, you have a gun. Reach for it."

"Don't! Don't!" whined the dope peddler. "I'll cut you in for half, I'll—"

"Reach for your gun," roared Pistolas and turned half around as if to watch Nick.

With a little scream of fear Tomas Serrano clawed at his armpit. A gun leaped half out before Juan Pistolas turned again. But before Serrano's automatic completely cleared its holster a shot rang out. Serrano leaped backward as if struck by a giant hand. Squarely between his eyes was a blue hole which rapidly reddened, began dripping grey and crimson. Juan Pistolas stood with a smoking, gold plated, heavy duty Colt in his right hand, the snarl of the killer on his face, the lust for murder in his black eyes.

He wheeled, listened at the door. From below the clatter was unbroken. Probably the gunshot would pass off as a blowout on the street.

"YOU," he said to the cowering, wide-eyed girl, "and you," to Papa Nick, still pasty with nausea, "are coming with me. Get up. Put that drape around you for clothes, *senorita*."

Wordlessly she obeyed.

"Face the wall," was the next low command. The two obeyed but over her shoulder Helen risked a look. Pistolas was crouched beside the dead body of Tomas Serrano, the hunchback. A knife flashed in his hand. Straight up the velvet *chaqueta*, the short ornate jacket, the knife slit its way. The silk shirt that covered the twisted hump was slashed. Helen Freeman's eyes widened, she heard Papa Nick grunt beside her as Juan Pistolas reached beneath the dead man's arms, fumbled for a moment then stood up grinning wolfishly with Tomas Serrano's hump dangling from severed straps in his right hand. Once more he leaned, slashed at the corpse once, twice, then straightened again. Helen Freeman leaned against the wall and retched.

"*Vamos,*" he grinned at the two.

There was a rear stairway that led to the kitchen. Down this clumped the strange procession, Papa Nick in the lead; his shaking hands high in the air, followed by white-faced Helen Freeman, a dirty curtain wrapped about her in lieu of a dress.

Joe Poblano was tucking the last of an enormous *tamale* between his gaping, thick lips. It thudded to the greasy plate before him; his chair fell over with a crash. His little eyes laid on his cheekbones.

"*Madre de Dios,*" he gasped.

Juan Pistolas grinned, stopped the procession. He threw the nondescript black hat into a corner, waved the gold plated pistol.

"For a long time, *amigo,*" he said softly, "you have wondered who I am. Do you know now? Look well!"

Poblano's voice seemed to have fled him. It came falteringly, hesitantly. "You are—you are—"

"Jose Maria Guedea Gardenia!"

"The Sabinas Kid!" Joe Poblano sat down weakly on the floor. He had forgotten the chair was no longer there. But he gazed up at the famous outlaw without moving.

"You are to take a message to Dr. Howard Murray, *amigo,* when I am gone. You are to tell him that the Sabinas Kid has ridden away with the hump of Tomas Serrano. Do not forget, *the hump of Tomas Serrano.* And you are to give him these."

He laid two bloody objects on the kitchen table. Joe Poblano turned even pastier.

"Tell him they are the ears of Tomas, and I shall have others for him before morning. Tell him that and do not forget. He will understand. Get going, the two of you."

The door slammed. A Ford roared in the alley and died away to nothingness before fat Joe could struggle to his feet. Beneath his breath he was

muttering "*Madre de Dios.* The Sabinas Kid rides again!"

EIGHT blocks from the international bridge the dark bulk of the abandoned ice house loomed bleak in the darkness. A Ford with no headlights drew to a stop before it. A fat figure was prodded from the Ford, sprawled on its face and began praying in three languages. A woman alit beside him to be followed by the driver, a lithe shadow with something gleaming ominously in his brown hand. In single file they entered the deserted building. From the back room a horse whinnied at the sound of his masters' step.

"Quiet, Diablo," said the Sabinas Kid softly and lighted a smoky lantern. Weird shadows were cast on the wall. In spite of Papa Nick's prayers and tears he was forced into a crumbling ice vault and the door slammed shut. The Sabinas Kid extracted tobacco and papers, began fashioning a cigarette.

"Now, *senorita,*" he spoke respectfully, "what is this I hear that you are spy? Have you learned of this doctor, this Murray?"

Instead of answering, she moved toward him. "Are you really the Sabinas Kid?"

He laughed, "To you I am only Juan Pistolas, the dishwasher. Answer my question."

"I won't lie to you; I couldn't!" Her hands were on his shoulders. Her mouth was strained, her eyes filled with intense yearning. The drape slid from her own rounded shoulders to disclose the upper slopes of milk-white breasts. "I'm no good, I guess. But a year ago I had a sister, as innocent as I am hard. I was working in a cabaret then, and sis got sick. I took her to Dr. Howard Murray and he prescribed for her. Before I knew it, she was a dope addict. Murray is a big man in the town, rich, society, plenty of friends. I couldn't prove anything. I knew he got his stuff through Papa Nick so I got myself a job there.

"My sister is dead now and I swore to avenge her death. That's all. I'd just found out that Serrano smuggled the stuff across the bridge somehow—you know the rest!"

She paused for a moment, eyes suddenly heavy. "Take me with you across the river," she breathed. Soft arms slid about his neck, her mouth was suddenly on his, her breasts flattening against his wide chest. For a moment he held her close, passion sweeping through his own hot Latin blood, then gently pushed her aside.

"Your story is almost mine," he said. "I loved a woman not long ago. When she grew ill, I brought her across the river to the *gringo*, Dr. Murray because he was famous, a big man. She came from his treatments a dope addict. Now she will do anything to get cocaine and heroin. I would have killed Murray here, but as you say he is a big man. I would have no chance of escape. If I can ever get him across the border into my country." His eyes grew contemplative. "But wait for me here. I will have work for you."

SHE waited wonderingly while he entered the crumbling ice vault that was the prison of Papa Nick. The walls were thick. But they did not keep the frantic screams of the fat Greek from the woman's listening ears. She shuddered deliciously, thought of the lithe pantherish body of the Sabinas Kid.

Presently he emerged, a blood-stained handkerchief in one hand, the lantern in the other. "Papa Nick," he said softly and his smile was wolfish, "doesn't feel like going back with you. You are to take this handkerchief to the office of Dr. Howard Murray and leave it on his desk when he is out. Lay this card beneath it." The little square of cardboard was neatly engraved with the words, "Compliments of Jose Maria Guedea Gardenia," and beneath it in flourishing long hand, "The Sabinas Kid."

"Take me with you," she breathed again, but he shook his head.

"I have a plan," he said. For long moments he talked while she nodded her head in understanding.

Ten minutes later she sat in the Ford looking out across the river. Only faintly could she make out a moving figure nearly half across the dark water. Her heart ached as she saw the black horse pull into the shallows, make the clump of trees on the opposite bank and disappear into their blackness. She started the car.

Two days later Julian the *Jorobado*, the hunchback, made his first appearance as a vendor of sweets on the streets of the little Mexican border town. His hair was uncombed and his face several shades darker than that of the Sabinas Kid. His hands seemed to shake with some nervous disorder and at times his black eyes were definitely crossed.

A strap spanned the huge hump on his back and supported the tray of candies. In spite of his vile appearance Julian the *Jorobado* was a cheerful soul. People bought his candy and pinched his bony hump three times for luck. Julian never objected but grinned in evident pleasure.

JULIAN had one fault; he loved *tequila*. Every night he spent his profits in some cafe, usually Mamasita Avila's where danced the glamorous

Conchita for the amusement of the *gringo* tourists who came nightly.

Conchita the Flame she was once called. Conchita was still a flame as a dancer but her freshness, her beauty was gone. Her eyes were mad now rather than lustrous, her legs too slender rather than full and shapely. It is a hard thing for a dope addict to make enough money to satisfy the craving.

Once she swayed by the tiny booth where Julian the *Jorobado* sat with his *tequila* bottle and her skirt swirled high about her once luscious hip. Julian shuddered a little as his eye caught the indisguisable mark of hundreds of tiny pits extending from knee to thigh—the mark of hypodermic needles. Julian poured himself a big drink and cursed Dr. Howard Murray and Tomas Serrano and Papa Nick and all men mixed up in the nasty traffic of drugs.

Several nights later he watched her dance again and his heart was heavy. He remembered that not so long ago he had loved this woman, that he had known the exquisite bloom of her passion, the breathless flame of her lips and body against his. Instinct warned him, but unable to resist as she danced past, he made a peculiar sign with his fingers. She hesitated, almost stopped her wild abandoned dance, but managed to continue to the end. When the

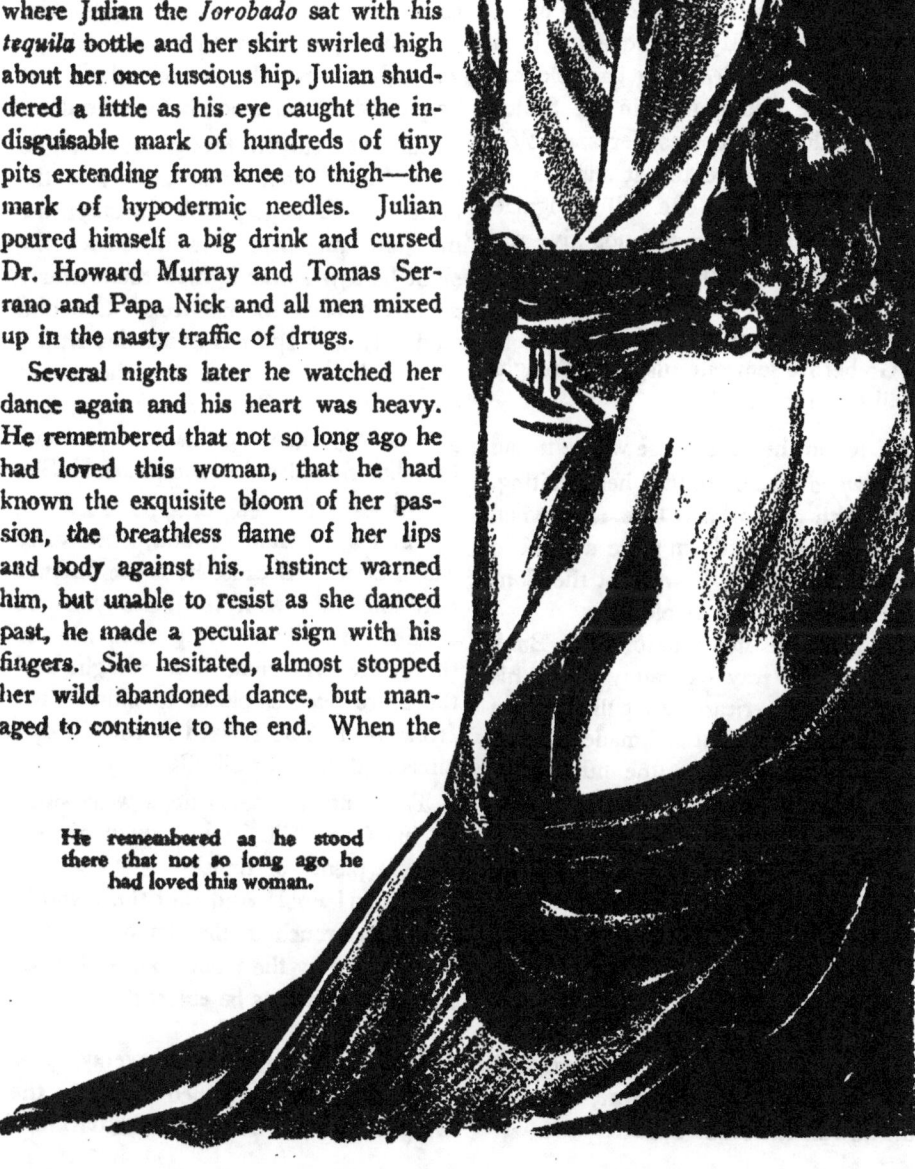

He remembered as he stood there that not so long ago he had loved this woman.

music stopped she slipped into the seat beside him.

"You come from him?"

He said, "Look closely, little flower," and laid his hat on the bench. She gasped, clutched her bosom.

"Chema! Jose! You have come back!" Love, passion, flared in her nervous eyes only to be replaced by a cunning look. "But you must not stay! Only today I see a new reward poster for you. Five thousand *pesos* they offer, dead or alive! My friend who is a lieutenant of the *Federales* has told me that you are also wanted in the States for the killing of Tomas Serrano! You must get out of here and at once!"

He grinned. "No one will recognize me. And surely you will not give me away." His eyes burned into hers. A look of fear swept her face.

"Not I! Never! But—"

"Go before someone suspects. Tonight I will come to you."

HE found the little house where it had always been, found her waiting, warm with passion and love. But when he left the place at dawn there was a bad taste in his mouth. It was not the Conchita he had known of old.

At noon he stood before the Bank Building, his tray of candy about his neck. An American car pulled up, a slender blonde got out and made her way across the sidewalk to the hunchback. It was Helen Freeman. She pretended to look through his tray of sweets.

"You have succeeded?" said the Sabinas Kid beneath his breath.

"I think so," she answered softly. "Tonight I will bring him. He has agreed to see you but he is very much afraid. Where will you be?"

"At Mamasita Avila's *cantina*. Tell him there is nothing to fear. Promise him he can handle it himself."

Helen nodded, paid for her candy and went back to the machine. Julian the *Jorobado* smiled to himself—the smile of the wolf. Tonight he meant to get the ears of this Dr. Howard Murray!

Darkness came. Whistling beneath his breath Julian shambled off toward Conchita's little house. He would tell her the news, tell her that he was about to avenge her. Then he would put her in an institution where that filthy habit could be cured! She had promised him only the night before that she would go willingly. A half block from the house he paused. A car stood before the door.

Suspicion surged through him. Whose car? Like a shadow he sulked to the back of the house, stole through the mesquite and close to a window. The sight he saw in the lighted room nearly sent him back to his heels. Conchita clad only in a short chemise was sitting on the skinny lap of a lanky lieutenant of *Federales!* He was caressing her possessively, running his hands across her slim shoulder, her round arms. She pulled away pouting.

"You are afraid of him," her voice was a taunt. "Because he is the Sabinas Kid and fast with his guns you are afraid to face him. Well, then, why do that? He will come here tonight and there are bushes, places to hide in the front yard. The reward is for the Sabinas Kid, dead or alive."

The lieutenant stood up, a weak smile on his face. "I'll have a squad of men here in plenty of time."

"Squad! Fool! And split the reward? You can crouch in the shadow of that mango tree by the front door and shoot him in the back as he enters!"

THERE was more controversy. The Sabinas Kid grinned beneath the window and slid away into the darkness cursing the drug that could change a sweetheart into a betrayer.

About nine that evening a *muchacho* slid into the *cantina* and told Julian the Jorobado that an *Americano* wanted him outside. Conchita who was sitting with him seized his hand. "You will come tonight?" Her eyes were veiled, her breasts heaved as if in anticipation.

"*Si*," grinned the Sabinas Kid, "the Jorobado will be there."

A long black sedan was parked by the curb. Helen Freeman was at the wheel. Doctor Howard Murray sat in the back seat and Taylor the ranchman sat beside the woman who drove. Both held guns in their hands.

"Get in," said Murray curtly and the Sabinas Kid got in beside him. They drove off into the night, engaged in low conversation.

"You mistake me, *senor*," protested the Kid. "I kill Serrano because I want his end of the business. There is much money to be made here. I have contacted the man who can supply us and I will send you to him, although he is very difficult to reach. You can make your own deal with him and I will be your messenger, the man who delivers it, just as Tomas Serrano used to do. Will you go alone to see this man?"

Murray growled, "How do I know it isn't a trick of some kind? Why should I trust you?"

The Sabinas Kid shrugged. "Taylor can sit in the car and hold a gun on me. Besides I am placing my life in your hands. I am the Sabinas Kid and there is a great reward for me, dead or alive. What more can you ask? Should anything go wrong Taylor has only to turn me over to the *Federales*."

"What am I supposed to do? How do I see this man?"

"The sign is the sign of the hump.

A humpbacked man is to meet him at midnight. You shall take my hump, my coat, and my sombrero and go yourself. In the darkness no one will tell you from me. Once inside you can explain who you are and I will give you my ring to prove that you come from me."

A LITTLE after midnight the dark sedan slid to a stop a full half block from the house of Conchita. A strangely humped figure got out of the back seat, spoke to Taylor who held a gun on the man who remained in the tonneau. "Taylor, I don't like this much but I'm going to take a chance. If I'm not back in fifteen minutes drive this Mex into town and turn him over to the *Federales*. Tell them it's the Sabinas Kid.

"Do not forget, senor," the soft voice of the Kid, "to whistle a few bars of *Rancho Grande* softly as you approach. It is to be the signal. Show them my ring and they will know you are from me."

Murray grunted and swung off into the blackness. The Sabinas Kid lit a cigarette leaned back in the tonneau and waited.

Conchita heard the low whistle approaching the house. She opened the door swiftly, listened a moment then hissed, "He comes! Get ready! When I open the door so he is in the light, shoot him."

Behind the mango tree the sweating lieutenant looked to his automatic, breathed a prayer to his patron saint. This Sabinas Kid might be a hard one to kill!

The humpbacked figure turned hesitantly into the path that led to the house. For a moment he paused, peering at the lighted window, then whistling boldly he went forward.

(Continued on page 114)

The WOMAN of CAYENNE

*In the jungles of French Guiana the Tumbleweed
meets death more than half-way, and learns once more
that his fatal weakness is believing too much in women*

A FEW men knew Neale as the Tumbleweed, but it was he who had dubbed himself by that sobriquet. Like a tumbleweed of his native prairies, blown hither and thither on the winds of chance. Neale had done many things that he hated to remember, but it was a certain strain of idealism in his nature, a naive belief in human goodness, and especially in women, that had been primarily his undoing.

In his reflective moments he recognized that fact with amusement. If he had been wholly bad, he would have got a good deal more out of life than he had done. Especially more than he was doing now.

For Neale was down and out, and in

When he saw big Pieters there, for a moment his mind went blank.

By HUGH SPEER

Cayenne, French Guiana, of all places in the world. He had come back to civilization after living for six months in the hut of an Indian woman, far in the interior, who had nursed him back to life when he was half dead with a stab wound in the back. And Neale hated to think of that, because she had loved him in her savage way.

And yet, what else could he have done? He couldn't have brought Amarawa into a civilized town. And she had her lovers. She had betrayed him good and plenty—for red-skinned blowpipe experts of the jungle. Neale had known all about that, and accepted it in the ironic spirit in which he looked upon life.

SIX weeks afoot, tramping from the interior to Cayenne, and here he was broke, ragged, and drunk on good French brandy that a trader on the out-

skirts had given him two or three hours before. The Tumbleweed had three francs in his pocket. Oh, it was one of the Tumbleweed's bad periods!

He had nothing in view. He was walking, with a rather staggering gait, along the seafront, between rows and rows of houses, from whose windows half-caste women, Indian women, Chinese, Japanese, and negro women whispered and beckoned to him.

A girl stepped out of a doorway and planted herself before him. A slender girl, not more than twenty, with plump breasts swelling and undulating beneath the thin cotton garment that she wore. An outline of brown thighs, and a woman's body that could cling close to a man desolate for comfort, and soothe him into peace and quiescence, make him a man again, in place of an outcast.

"You come with me, sailor," whispered the girl, putting a slim brown hand on the Tumbleweed's ragged arm.

What was she? Part French, part Indian, part Japanese, perhaps, one of those rare beauties that cross-breeding sometimes throws up. A girl to bring a man comfort, to hold him in her arms. And there was a lot of the child in Neale. And just now he was down and out and friendless.

"*Pas d'argent*. No money," muttered the Tumbleweed.

The girl surveyed him critically. "*Mon Chér*, you have been sick. Me, yes, I understand. Come with me and forget."

The Tumbleweed shook his head and staggered away. He didn't know just why. But he had three francs in his pocket, and his immediate need was the two drinks of cheap spirits that those three francs would bring him.

AT THE next corner he saw the "Mouton d'Or," a sailors' dive, a gaudy place by the waterfront, with a radio blaring and a crowd of all colors and nationalities inside. Neale went in and sat down at a little table. He barked an order for absinthe to the half-breed waitress, who looked at his rags with a sneer she did not take the trouble to conceal.

Neale looked about him, at the cosmopolitan crowd, sailors dancing with waterfront wenches in their arms, drunken men wrangling, women frankly soliciting, and pointing to rooms behind the curtain at the rear.

And then Neale saw big Pieters stalk out of his office and survey the crowd, and for a moment his mind went blank. For he hadn't dreamed Pieters would be there, as the proprietor of this hell-hole in Cayenne.

NEALE lived through months in that moment, in accordance with the queer laws of the mind. He was back, six months before, at Iraqui, far in the interior, where a score of prospectors, French, English, Dutch, were working the gravel of a river-bed in the hope of duplicating a diamond find that had recently been made.

Blue mud, that turned yellow as it disintegrated, sure sign of volcanic diamond deposits, a few small finds, and a score of tents and huts run up by the prospectors. All about them, densest jungle, and on one side the river, their only means of intercourse with the world outside.

War with the savage denizens of that jungle, because big Pieters and two or three others had gone to a native village and attacked some of the girls.

Poisoned arrows shot through blow-pipes, sudden, treacherous attacks by night, constant patrolling, now and again the crack of a rifle, and some sneaking Indian tumbling headlong from his ambush beside the trail. Word had been sent to the nearest French post, and rescue was expected.

And, in their hut, Neale's partner, the young American, Collins, dying of malignant fever. Just one chance in a thousand for his recovery.

Just a nice boy from Kansas, with whom Neale had joined in the diamond prospecting expedition.

Neale nursed him, and patrolled the fields at night, when the natives sneaked up with their deadly blowpipes, and slept when he could snatch an hour or two.

Collins had found a diamond, yellow, but of great size and purity. A nice little sum of money; but they hoped it was only the prognostication of better things to come. They had kept the news from big Pieters, the Dutchman. He was the bully of the camp. It was Pieters who had provoked the war that had turned the diamond fields into an intrenched camp.

Collins was babbling of his young wife. A French girl, daughter of an old Major in charge of the convict settlement. Collins had never before told Neale of the romance that had culminated in a secret marriage three months earlier.

"We loved each other so much," he whispered. "If her father knew, he'd turn her out of his house. He hates Americans. And we loved each other."

They had spent two furtive days and nights together before Collins started for the diamond fields, Neale learned from Collins' babblings.

"You'll be well soon, partner," said the Tumbleweed, "and we'll go back to Cayenne with a fortune big enough to soften the old man's heart."

But he knew Collins would not recover. And Collins was back in his delirium, babbling of those nights with Geneste. Muttering things that Neale had no right to know. About her passionate needs, and her suppression of them throughout the period of her schooldays in France. They had been everything to each other, it appeared.

Rare, thought Neale, in this ironic fashion. Rare that two beings, plunged into a romantic marriage, should find this utter satisfaction in each other.

"Cheer up, old man," said Neale. "Your temperature's down two degrees."

But he knew that it was down because Collins was dying.

SHOUTS from the watchers brought Neale out of the hut at dawn.

A boat was coming down the Iraqui. A boat in which a woman sat, paddled by four natives.

A white woman. A woman with yellow hair—a girl, wearing a short skirt and blouse, absurdly out of place in that steaming, fly-infested jungle, where the body and each limb was encased in stiff khaki for protection.

A girl of about twenty-two, with a mass of bobbed yellow hair falling about her face, small, rounded breasts, hardly as mature as a woman's, pointing through the blouse, slender hips and slim legs encased in brown topboots.

A dozen miners gathered at the landing-place to meet her as she stepped ashore.

"I am Madame Collins," she said in voluble French. "I have come to see my husband."

They stared at her, big Pieters stroking his beard and licking his thick lips. To these men, accustomed to the company of the brown native girls, the sight of a white woman was like champagne.

Neale stepped forward. But, before he could speak, she chattered on:

"You see, we were married three months ago, and my father died last month, leaving me alone. So I had to come to see my husband. They told me there was trouble with the natives, but I had to come—you understand, I had to come."

"I am afraid, madame," said Neale, "your husband is very sick. We are sharing the same hut. Let me take you to him."

She glanced at Neale in dismay, but said nothing. Only, when she put her little hand on Neale's arm, something within the Tumbleweed leaped into life. Desire—passion, romance, the sense that at last he had met the one woman of his life.

Neale led her to the hut in which Collins lay, babbling his life away. With a cry, the girl threw herself upon her knees beside him.

"Charles, I am Geneste. Do you not know me, sweetheart?" she cried in French.

No, Charles Collins didn't know her, and he would never know her. He lay there, breathing heavily and muttering. There was a cord about his neck, and upon his chest was the great yellow uncut diamond.

Geneste rose to her feet and looked at Neale. Neale couldn't meet her eyes, but he knew she understood.

He went out, leaving her with the dying man.

A S HE left the hut, yells sounded from the jungle. There followed the crackle of firearms. Neale saw men running toward the river, and little brown men debouching from the river thickets. Dozens of them, scores of them. The Indians were attacking in force. A shower of arrows hurtled through the air. Two of the white miners dropped. For the moment the whites were being forced back.

Neale ran forward, firing his automatic. A native dropped. He shot another squarely between the eyes as he was placing his infernal blowpipe to his lips. He picked up one of the fallen miners in his arms, then saw that he was already dead, shot through the throat. The second man was on his feet, staggering weakly.

Neale put his arm around him, thrust a new clip of cartridges into his weapon, emptied it into the yelling hordes that were advancing.

Then a half-dozen of the whites were at his side, big Pieters among them, and a storm of bullets drove the assailants back into the cover of the jungle.

With his arm about the wounded man, the Tumbleweed returned to the shelter of the entrenched camp. All through that day they waited, but the attack was not renewed.

Amarawa cooked them food in the kitchen hut. She was pure Indian, a little, lithe, slim-flanked girl with small, delicate breasts bare above her cotton skirt, and flashing brown thighs that drew the gaze of the woman-hungry men of the mining camp. Amarawa was naively generous and loved with childish simplicity all who sought her.

And Amarawa had been Neale's undoing. When he disengaged himself from her arms, the pity of it, and the reverence for womanhood that had always been his undoing, struck him like a blow between the eyes.

That had been six weeks before. Amarawa had often flashed him an inviting look in passing, but he had never sought her company again.

He felt no immediate pain. He didn't
know why his mouth and nostrils were
suddenly suffused with blood.

Two or three times during the day Neale looked in at his hut, but Collins now lay in the final stupor that precedes death, and Geneste sat beside him, apparently crushed by the tragedy of it.

Night had fallen, with the suddenness of the tropics, when Neale went back. The hut was dark, but he could see Geneste faintly outlined against the little window, and Collins lying on his back, silent now. He went up to the dying man, placed his hand upon his forehead, and felt the sweat there. He turned toward Geneste.

He was trying to formulate some words of condolence. He realized the tragedy of that long, useless journey of hers. But before he could speak, the girl had come forward.

SHE HAD undressed. Neale hadn't realized that, but now he saw her clothes in a little pile upon his own bunk. She had on her shoes and stockings, and a wrapper that swung open at the waist, shadowedly revealing the small breasts and tapering arms, and the white hips that seemed to gleam in the moonlight.

"How is he?" Neale asked, because he couldn't think of anything less commonplace to say.

"He is dying, and we have known it," answered Geneste, moving closer to Neale, so that the fragrance of her caught his senses. Her bare arms were upon his shoulders, and her breasts lifted and slid against the thin material of her wrapper.

Six weeks since that episode with Amarawa. Six weeks' devotion to an ideal, on the part of the poor Tumbleweed, and now this girl was all but in his arms, pulsating with ecstasy; and then her arms were around his neck, and

her warm, moist lips were quivering upon his.

And Collins, Neale's friend and partner, and her husband, dying in the same cabin, beginning the last irregular, gasping breathing that Neale knew so well.

"My dear, I can't—I can't," Neale muttered, detaching her arms from about his neck. He pressed back against one breast, involuntarily feeling its warmth, as if that fleshly instinct was something apart from him, some monster trying to control him.

"Listen," she panted. "I—I don't know how many other women are like me, but I was—made for love. All my life, since I was a tiny child, I needed it. And he awakened me to understanding. We were married just two days and nights. *Mon dieu*, do you not understand the torture I have been through without him? And the long trip up the river, with the Indian boatmen, when I remembered that I was a white woman and—Ah, they were strong, handsome men, but, you see, I am a white woman, and I have been a good woman. Yes, a true wife. And now he is dying, and I—want you, Neale."

"No, my dear, a man doesn't do that —not like this," answered Neale. And at that moment Collins' heavy breathing began to cut through the air, horrible, heavy breathing, the last struggle of the physical organism against the inevitability of death.

For a moment longer she stood face to face with Neale, and the warmth of her breast was still against him, despite himself, and he was mad to take her in his arms, even in that cabin of death.

Then he pushed her away. She recoiled against the bunk. She said, quite softly:

"Very well, Neale. You have done more than you know. Go away, then!

Go away! Leave me, and never come back!"

Neale went out of the hut.

YELLS sounded from the jungle. Rifles and automatics were cracking. The Indians were attacking again. They had stolen up under cover of darkness, and were pouring in arrows and blowpipe darts from the other side of the low entrenchments, which were thinly manned by the defenders.

In that night attack it was each man for himself. Neale raged to and fro, firing at the dark shapes that came leaping forward, encouraging the defenders. He saw three men go down with blowpipe dart wounds on their faces—tiny, weak missiles that would not pierce a man's clothing; and yet, within ten minutes, each of them had died an agonizing death. Once he saw something that obstructed his use of his weapon—something projecting from his shoulder; and he pulled out an arrow, which was followed by a gush of blood.

He flung it away and raged on, loading, firing and reloading, encouraging the little band of desperate white men, until the other side of the entrenchments was strewn with the fallen bodies of the savages, and the attack died away in utter silence. It was only then that it occurred to Neale big Pieters had not been in the fight.

The big Dutchman, bully though he was, and self-constituted ruler of the camp, was not a coward. Neale and Collins had never had any difficulty with him. There had been no love lost between them, but they had tacitly avoided conflict.

"Where's Pieters?" he asked someone.

The man shrugged his shoulders. Neale, tired to death, turned away, and made his way back to the cabin. He didn't feel like facing Geneste again, but Collins, his friend, was dying.

No, Collins was dead. He lay, with his face cold and white, upon his bunk, and a single glance was sufficient to tell Neale that the end had come.

Collins had died alone. At least, Geneste was not in the cabin, and the little pile of clothes was gone.

Neale felt a sudden fear for her. Where had she gone? Had she wandered away?

A shadow darkened the entrance of the cabin. At first Neale thought it was Geneste. But it was Amarawa, the Indian girl, with her lithe, brown body and small breasts — Amarawa, the camp's plaything, perhaps the camp's necessity, degraded and outcast, even among her own people, and yet come to perform the last rites for the dead man, as her first words disclosed.

"Where is the white woman?" Neale demanded.

Amarawa pointed toward a hut close by. Pieters' hut!

A sudden madness gripped the Tumbleweed. Had Pieters taken advantage of the fighting to bend Geneste to his will? If he had wronged her, Neale meant to kill him.

HE THRUST the Indian girl aside and staggered out into the darkness. He felt himself reeling, and realized that he had been fighting all day and all night; Neale was almost at the end of his resources of physical energy.

Big Pieters lived alone, in a round hut adjoining the long sorting table on which he spread out the blue diamond ore to disintegrate into yellow mould under the influence of the sunlight. Neale entered the sorting-hut, with its crude roof, and pushed open the packing-case door of Pieters' cabin. As he entered, he heard a sound that made him stop still, frozen with horror.

It was the soft sighing of a woman, the soft, quick, sighing, panting breathing of a woman held in a man's arms.

In that moment the poor Tumbleweed went through all the agonies of hell. For he had loved Collins, the little Kansas boy, with all his unworldly, boyish faith in life, in honor, in women, and he had idealized Geneste, even in spite of the gust of passion that had swept her off her feet. Now he could dimly descry her, suddenly muted with appeased desire, lying in the big Dutchman's arms.

Neither of them seemed to have heard him when he called:

"Come out, Pieters. I'm going to kill you!"

There was a scream. Geneste was upon her feet before Pieters had lumbered to his. She was standing before Neale, clad in a single, gossamer garment, from which one small breast half protruded. He could see the outlines of her hips, the white knees and lower limbs beneath the garment's hem, and the little arched feet planted upon the earthen floor.

"Your husband is dead," said Neale, hearing an odd choke in his voice. "He's lying dead in our cabin, and I find you here with this man!"

"No, no, you must be merciful!" she screamed. "I told you. I warned you. I couldn't go on living the way I had. I—I—"

Big Pieters thrust aside and came leaping at Neale, fists whirling. Neale put all his strength into a right-handed blow that sent the Dutchman staggering back. He followed with a left that knocked him flat upon the mud floor.

"Get up." he said, and now his voice was a soft, moaning whine. "I'm going to kill you with my hands, you dog!"

Geneste had suddenly grown silent. She had drawn back into the shadows of the cabin. Pieters got on his feet. Neale thought he heard the woman muttering to the big man, but he wasn't sure—he wasn't sure of anything, save that little Collins lay dead in the hut, and that his wife had betrayed him.

Big Pieters shambled forward. "Come outside," he mumbled thickly. "I'll skin you, Neale. I'll—"

Then it was that the woman rushed. Rushed, screaming. Neale felt her fist impact against his back. But he didn't know that there were four inches of steel protruding from it.

He felt no pain. He didn't know why his mouth and nostrils were suddenly suffused with blood. He didn't know why it was so difficult to breathe, and why he was falling forward, stumbling, clutching at the empty air.

Then he was down, still not understanding that he had three inches of steel in his left lung. But his rage had suddenly burned out, and the poor Tumbleweed was very, very tired.

HE DIDN'T faint. He just pitched forward upon the threshold between the hut and the sorting-room, and lay there. As if in a dream, he heard Geneste crying:

"I've killed him! *Ah, mon dieu,* what shall we do?"

"I'm going to throw him down in the jungle," answered Pieters. "The Indians will finish him off. Nobody will ever know."

"Poor boy!" moaned Geneste. "Ah, the poor boy. He was so innocent! I hate you!" she cried in sudden fury.

"You can go on hating me all you want to, my dear, but we've got to save our necks," answered big Pieters.

The hard light in her eyes now was
that of a damned soul.

Neale was vaguely aware of being
raised in the big man's arms and carried
through the darkness. Pieters slipped
and stumbled over the entrenchments,
recovered himself, went on into the
jungle. At last Neale felt himself
dropped into the scrub beside the river.
And with that consciousness went out.

AFTERWARD he calculated that
days must have gone by before he
came back to consciousness in Amarawa's hut. And it was days more before

she made him understand, in her mixture of Indian, French, and English, that the troops had arrived and taken the prospectors away by boat.

She had come upon him, lying in the jungle, she said, though Neale always suspected she had been a witness of the whole scene. She had taken him to her lonely hut and cared for him, dressing his wound with herbs she gathered from the forests, bringing him back to life when he was at death's very door.

When Neale looked back afterward upon those months in the hut of the Indian girl, it seemed to him that they were a wonderful interlude in his life. At first she mothered him as if he had been a child. There was her soft shoulder on which to place his head at night, there were her arms to hold him. It was long, long before Neale came to the physical consciousness of her as a woman, lovely and desirable.

For time and again death reached out a skinny claw and sought to engulf him, and time and again he was brought back to life by Amarawa, the outcast, the camp's plaything, the high priestess of humanity.

At last there came the time when Neale's strength had come back to him, and then he remembered that he was a man.

Two or three months went by. He was strong again and well now, and day by day he knew more surely that he would be forced to come to the inevitable decision.

Amarawa had already been deceiving him with the red men of the district, because, like a child, she was incapable of self-control, and because she knew nothing of the white man's ways. If he left here, there would be tears and wretchedness for a brief spell, and then she would find consolation.

And it was unthinkable to take this jungle girl into Cayenne. She would wilt and die there.

"I'm going back to my own people," he said one day. And added, lying, "Perhaps I'll return some day."

"You will never return," answered the girl. "I know the ways of the white man."

That last night, holding Amarawa in his arms, the Tumbleweed attained a clearer understanding of women than he had ever reached before—their faithlessness, their tenderness, their inconstancy and their loyalty. He knew that those months with Amarawa would leave their mark with him for ever. And a mark that would not wholly be a scar.

His last memory of her was seeing her waving to him from her hut as he stepped out along the jungle trail that ran toward Cayenne.

NEALE'S mind cleared. He was sitting at the table in the Mouton d'Or, looking at big Pieters in his flashy suit, with the rings upon his fingers. Pieters had evidently prospered since he opened the "Mouton d'Or."

And then he saw Geneste. She was sitting at a table with two drunken sailors, and, apparently dissatisfied with their offer, she rose with a shrug of her shoulders and paraded down the room.

In the six months that had passed she had changed immeasurably. She was fattened, bloated, coarsened, though she still retained something of her girlish charm and beauty. But the hard light in her eyes was that of a damned soul.

She saw Neale as he sat in the shadows, and swaggered up to him, with bold, trembling breasts and swaying hips.

"'Ello, sailor!" she challenged him.

"You want to make friend with me, yes?"

She didn't recognize the ragged, emaciated Tumbleweed as the friend of her husband. Neale nodded and rose.

Geneste led Neale past Pieters, who was looking the other way, along a passage with doors on either side, from behind which came the sounds of men's voices and women's·tinkling laughter. Into a small room near the end, Geneste turned toward Neale casually, and loosed the straps from her shoulders. The little breasts, larger now, and less firm, but still desirable, were partly revealed as the dress fell apart.

" 'Ow you like me, sailor?" asked Geneste.

Neale looked at her steadily, and saw the sudden recognition, the sudden horror come into her eyes.

"*Ah mon dieu*, you! But you are dead!"

"I didn't die," said the Tumbleweed. "And I don't want you, Geneste. I came, just to see you, for the sake of old times. For the sake of my dead friend," he went on bitterly.

Suddenly she sank down at his feet, clutching at his knees. "Neale, Neale," she sobbed, "if I 'ad known you were alive, this would not 'ave 'appen to me. I am bad woman now, and yet I am the daughter of a French officer."

Neale was silent.

"You can never forgive? You cannot remember what I said to you? I wanted you. I told you you had done more than you knew. If you had taken me, there would have been no Pieters, and I should never 'ave been what I 'ave become. Forgive me, for the sake of the man we both loved."

Neale was still silent. He was thinking of Amarawa, of her tenderness and her treachery. All women were the same.

"See, Neale, I tell you something. That diamond that you and Collins found—I 'ave it. I 'ave hidden it. Pieters does not know about it. It is in my stocking. Take me away, Neale. Take me to your own country. I will be true to you."

"I don't want my share of the diamond," answered Neale, "and I don't want you."

A man's steps stopped in the doorway. Neale looked up and saw big Pieters.

"I thought I reckernized you, sailor," said Pieters. "You was at Iraqui, wasn't you? Sure, sure, the friend of Geneste's sweetheart. I'm glad she didn't kill you."

There was not a trace of malice in his tone. Memories are short in the Guianas, where death treads so swiftly upon the heels of life.

"YOU look as if you're up against it, boy," Pieters went on. "This place is yours, and Geneste—well, maybe you still like her company, huh?"

"Ah, you beast, you brute! *Mon dieu*, I hate you!" wailed Geneste. "Neale, take me away, Neale. I'll be so true. Trust me!"

The dress had slid down still further, revealing the smooth curves of her breasts. Even then, Neale was conscious of the stirrings of desire in him as he looked at her. A beautiful woman, even though she was every drunken sailor's, so long as he had money.

But Neale was thinking of young Collins, babbling of the wife he had left behind him, of young Collins, lying cold in death, and Geneste in big Pieters' arms.

(*Continued on page 109*)

DESERT

By SAM WALSER

THE LAZY hum of ancient Tebessa's streets was only a faint echo in the little Barbary room, with its gilded ornaments and woollen rugs, where Wild Bill Clanton scowled down at the girl who stretched with feline abandon on the couch beside which he stood.

Clanton was a broad-shouldered, hard-fisted, lean-waisted American whose face was browned by the suns of the Seven Seas. It was not the first time he had come to Tebessa on business not to be shouted from the house-tops, but it was the first time he had been confronted by a situation like this, while mingling a little pleasure with his business.

"What the hell?" he demanded of the world at large, and particularly of the girl who smiled up at him with mocking

BLOOD

*"The man I love must be a slayer of lions," the lovely
Algerian girl had said. And Wild Bill Clanton's vanity
wouldn't let him let well enough alone*

malice. "What's the matter with you,
Zouza?"

She twisted over on her supple stomach and propped herself on her elbows.
There was no veil to hide her roguish
features, her full, pouting lips and *kohl-*

"There are
ways of persuasion," she
said, dangerously.

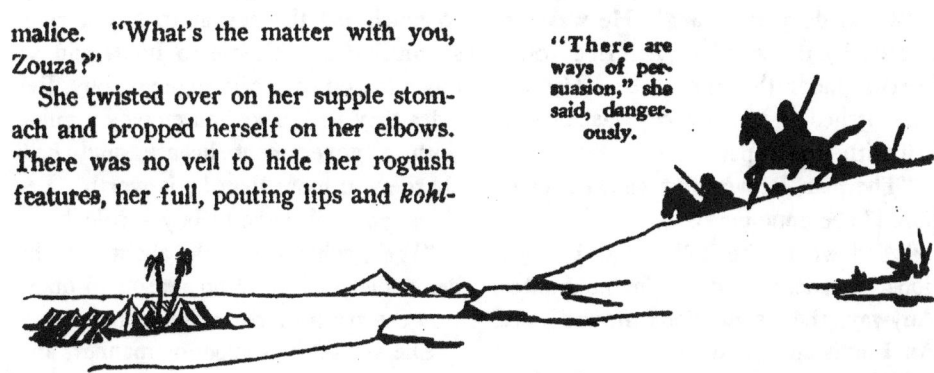

darkened lids, which now drooped amusedly over dark eyes that sparkled with hidden meaning. Her *gandourah*, the robe worn by Algerian women, was a filmy wisp through which shone the warm ivory flesh beneath. Her broad girdle, drawn close about her supple waist, outrageously emphasized the contours of her ripe hips as she lay there, one leg thrust out in a straight line, the other kicking up a trim heel in the feminine joy of tantalizing a male, so the little crimson slipper barely clung to one saucy toe.

"Women love valiant men!" she asserted.

"Nobody ever called me a coward," he growled. He was puzzled. He had been in Tebessa a week, and had fallen in with her the first day. There had been nothing elusive about her then. She had bestowed upon him enough of the flavor of her exuberant charms to rouse in him an imperative thirst for more. But business had intervened then, and he had been unable to see her again until today. And now she repulsed him.

Moreover it was easy to see that she was not prompted by a mere coquettish whim, rising from a desire to be deliciously mastered, after a mock resistance. He chafed, puzzled and angry.

"You fight men!" she mocked. "Have you fought beasts—the king of beasts?"

"What do you mean?" He was fascinated by the swell of her ripe young breasts under the filmy robe. His fingers itched. Impatience was playing hell with his temper.

"The man I love must be a slayer of lions!" she announced.

"And where the hell would I slay a lion?" he demanded. "I'm no hunter. Anyway, there's no lions around here. An Englishman told me—"

"*That* for your accursed English-man!" she interrupted with an inelegant but descriptive gesture. "There are lions in the forest of Alloufa, one day's ride from Tebessa. If you were a brave man—"

"SHUT up!" he yelled, stung to the quick. He had never faced a lion, it was true, but his mallet-like fists had impacted on human jaws from Frisco to Singapore, alike on ship's decks and in sea-port saloons, and his was the natural vanity of a fighting man. Mingling with his hunger to crush this saucy bit of warm, scented flesh in his arms, there rose a pugnacious urge to answer this challenge to his manhood. No strong man can endure being jeered at for cowardice by the woman he desires. Circumstances had enforced a postponement of the culmination of his business in Tebessa. He felt he could safely devote the next few days to his personal affairs.

"All right! But I'll have to get a guide, and a license or permit or somethin', won't I?" A man of the sea, his ideas of landsmen's rules and regulations were extremely hazy. Zouza bent her head to hide a triumphant smile; this hard-fisted bucko was as wax in her small hands.

"The authorities will rob you," she announced. "They will make you pay so much for the permit to buy a rifle, so much for a license to hunt, and so much tax on each cartridge you buy. Besides they will make you employ a guide with a government license, and *he'll* charge you more than he is worth. Besides, you will have to buy a rifle."

"Well, what can I do about it?" he demanded. He had no reason to question the truth of her statements.

She smiled in a superior manner, and announced: "I will arrange it, and it will cost you nothing! I have a cousin who is a famous lion hunter. He is Ahmed ibn Said. You have heard of him?"

"Naw."

"*Roumis* are without knowledge," she said loftily. "Never mind. Procure a donkey and at dusk ride alone out of the city, to the Well of Mansourah, three miles to the south. If any Frenchman sees you go, he will think you go to visit some woman of the Ouled-Nayl near the Well. But Ahmed will be waiting there with horses and a rifle. He will show you how to slay a lion unbeknownst to the French, Allah curse them!"

"How do you know I want to chase off to Alloufa just to shoot a lion for you?" he grumbled. "You're not the only skirt in Tebessa!"

"But I am Zouza!" she assured him, with the naive vanity that always amused and stimulated him. "You will prove yourself a man for me!"

And with a gurgle of glee she rolled lithely on her back, kicking up her heels like a frolicsome filly, heedless of the resultant display of ivory flesh. The little red slippers flew across the room, and with a peal of silvery laughter she swung her bare legs out of Clanton's reach, snatched her robe away from his grabbing hands and sprang from the couch, taking refuge behind it.

"No, no, not yet! Not any more until you have heard *El Adrea* roar: '*Ana wa el-bin el-mera!*' Go now and do not come back until you have proved yourself a man!"

A FEW moments later Clanton, swearing under his breath, strode out into the streets and almost bumped into another woman, the very antithesis of Zouza. Instinctively he doffed his cap. He knew her—had met her at the consul's office in Constantine a few weeks before. She was Miss Augusta Evans, a New England school-teacher on vacation, and like all her breed of both sexes, prone to wander into all sorts of outlandish places.

The stare she returned him was frigid. Evidently she had a pretty good idea as to the nature of the place he had just left. She was handsome enough in a cold, reserved way. The riding-habit she wore displayed a well-rounded figure, and there was a wealth of light hair under the British sun-helmet New Englanders feel obliged to wear anywhere east of Gibralter. Her features were classical in their severe regularity, and easy to look at, in spite of the tight-lipped expression of disapproval she frequently wore, denoting her condemnation of anything that differed from the habits and traditions of Boston.

It was partly because of the curves betrayed by the close-fitting riding breeches, as well as an honest desire to be helpful to a fellow-countrywoman, which prompted Clanton to address the girl. After all, you never could tell.

"Good afternoon, Miss Evans," quoth he, his eyes focusing somewhere south of her waist-line. "I understand you're interested in archaeology. There's some Roman ruins a few miles south of town, that—"

Her voice dripped icicles as she answered.

"Thank you, Mr. Clanton, but I am quite aware of that fact. I assure you that I am in no need of your assistance. As a matter of fact, I am just now completing my plans for hiring a guide and exploring those ruins tomorrow. The consul warned me against you—he said you were suspected of being a gun-runner and worse, and the house you have just emerged from quite substantiates his opinion of you. Good day, Mr. Clanton!"

"Okay, sister!" Clanton left her instantly, smarting.

"Damn', prudified, stuck-up snip!" His tentative interest had been chilled, in spite of those tempting curves. His only emotion right now was a wish that he could give the fair owner of those enticing riding breeches a good spanking.

This incident, coming right on top of his maddeningly unsatisfactory interview with Zouza, left him in a state of extreme exasperation toward women in general. He found a boy with a donkey for hire, gave him some instructions, and then, still seething with resentment and frustration, he sought a certain house of entertainment, cleverly camouflaged by an innocent-appearing silk shop.

He was presently seated in a wide cellar, among a motley crew of cutthroats, watching the gyrations of half a dozen dancing girls who had just enough Soudanese blood in them to impart an untamed voluptuousness found only in mixed breeds. Tobacco smoke rose in a blue cloud, and he occasionally caught a reek that didn't need the confirmation of vacant faces and dilated eyes to tell him some of the men were smoking more than tobacco. The place was a *hashish* den also.

IT WAS a hell of a place for a white man to be, but Wild Bill Clanton was generally to be found in places where most white men ventured only at the risk of their lives. When he yelled for liquor, it was brought to him by a brown-skinned Somali girl with eloquent rolling eyes, whose short slit skirt, worn for the convenience of customers with curiosity and roving hands, gaped revealingly at each strutting step. She smiled meltingly on the white man, but Clanton, in his present mood, eyed her coldly and applied himself to the liquor.

None of the Moslems objected at the presence of the forbidden liquid among them. Indeed, they eyed it wistfully, and at his invitation, laid aside their coffee-cups and drank heartily at his expense.

"Good Muhammadans, yeah!" he snorted. "When the Prophet forbade wine, he didn't mention brandy; so they stuff their guts with it."

And so did he. He neither knew nor cared whether these men knew why he was in Tebessa. It was a cinch the French didn't know. He had come there to arrange with the agent of certain Berber chiefs for the delivering of a cargo of rifles, from a ship of which he was captain and sole owner, and which now lay anchored safely at a certain obscure island well off-shore.

Only today he had learned from the agent that it would be another week before it could be done. Clanton was playing a risky game, but there was more than money involved. He had a sincere sympathy for those mountain tribesmen, fighting for life and freedom against a ruthless European power.

The dancing girls, stimulated by the presence of a *Roumi*, outdid themselves in vigor and abandon. But Clanton, with images of Zouza and Miss Augusta Evans mingling chaotically in his brain, merely glowered. He sat and drank and drank and drank, moodily watching the brown girls as they capered and cavorted, shedding garment after garment as they frisked before him, until to his slightly glazed eyes they merged into a whirling phantasm, many-armed and many-legged.

Clanton swung with his left. The giant went down with a fractured jaw.

HE CAME to himself with an awareness of motion beneath him and a wind out of the desert blowing in his face. He blinked, spat, swore, and glared about him. Here were no brown girls, no drunken Arabs—not even any lights, except the crazily-rocking stars overhead. He was on a donkey and the donkey was carrying him over a rocky trail.

He tried to orient himself. He had drunk more than he intended, and the close atmosphere, reeking with *hashish* fumes, had proved overpowering. Evidently the owner of the donkey had, according to previous instructions, brought the beast to the silk-shop, and told the Arabs, those still sober enough to understand, that the *Roumi* had intended riding southward.

They must have lifted him into the saddle and led the donkey to the southern outskirts of the city, and then left him to the mercy of Allah and the jackass, which was characteristic of the Arabic nature. Some dim instinct, not altogether submerged, had made him cling to the saddle and boozily urge his steed southward. And naturally it had gotten off the road.

He pulled up and glanced at the stars. He was not exactly lost, insofar as he still knew in which direction lay the Mediterranean Ocean and the Sahara Desert. He knew he must be somewhere south of the city. But where lay the Well of Mansourah, he had no idea. The terrain was a succession of ridges, and he could not have seen the lights of Tebessa, even if it were within a few miles. And it was nearly midnight, according to the position of the stars!

Either he had left the city much later than he had intended, or else he had been riding for many hours. And he was supposed to meet Zouza's cousin at dusk!

"Hell's fire!" He had no natural ambition to hear *El Adrea* roar: "I and the woman's son!" among the cork-oaks of Alloufa; but it had been Zouza's ultimatum; and now doubtless Zouza's cousin had given him up in disgust, and he had lost the easiest way of accomplishing his set task.

He urged the jackass to the crest of the nearest ridge. From there he still could not see the city lights, but he did see a single, glow-worm sort of a light, winking off to the northwest. He headed toward it, and presently saw that the light was in a tent which stood on a small

flat with a low ridge to the north. There was only one tent; a horse nickered behind it. As he dismounted the tent flap was pulled aside and a slender figure was silhouetted against the glow. A soft voice called anxiously: "Ahmed! Ahmed ibn Said! Is it you?"

"No, it's his friend!" announced Clanton, striding out of the darkness.

The girl cried out and sprang back, but Clanton caught her wrist. The liquor fumes were still rising to his brain, just enough to make him reckless of consequences, and the sight of her supple figure outlined against the light had set hammers going in his temples.

"Don't be afraid," he soothed, following her into the tent as she backed away, trying to free her wrist. He spoke Arabic as she had done. "I'm a friend of Ahmed's cousin. I lost my way in the darkness."

THERE was no one in the tent but themselves. She was prettier than Zouza, a little taller, with the sweet suppleness of limb that belongs only to Bedouin girls. With her sleeveless, low-necked vest of embroidered silk, open in front and half revealing the twin ivory hemispheres that were her youthful breasts, and with her voluminous pantaloons, girdled at the waist and caught in at the ankles, she might have just stepped from a Bagdad *harim*. Her lips were full and red and passionate, her eyes dark and expressive. Her slim shoulders and naked arms had just that touch of frailty that is most appealing to a powerfully-muscled man.

Fascinated by his captive, Clanton turned her about, feasting his eyes on her supple figure. She squirmed uneasily under his scrutiny, making no attempt to cover her breasts, but twisting her legs nervously in their filmy coverings. The fabric of her pantaloons was so sheer that the soft white flesh gleamed through it. He glimpsed hints of piquant contours that set his already hot blood a-riot.

"Are you Ahmed's wife?" he wondered aloud. "His sister?"

A mute shake of the head answered each question; he understood the situation and grinned, relieved of any scruples he might otherwise have felt.

"And he leaves you here alone?"

"He went to meet a *Roumi* at the Well of Mansourah," she answered, finding voice at last. "No man would dare touch a woman of Ahmed ibn Said!"

Clanton grinned.

"Yeah? Well, I'm different!" Two broad hands reaching for her, pulling her toward him, removed any doubt on that score. Beneath the filmy covering her skin was velvety to his touch. She did not shrink from his caress, nor did she seek to draw away when his arm encircled her supple waist and drew her closer to him.

A warm light that was neither fear nor resentment began to glow in her dark eyes as, recovering from her first shock of surprise and fear, she began to take stock of the intruder.

Arab girls admire strength, and Clanton was overflowing with that; audacity, and nobody ever accused him of timidity. She met his gaze squarely, staring at his broad shoulders, deep chest, hard waist and thickly-muscled arms.

"If he should catch you in my tent he would kill you," she said. "He is a trusted man of Shaykh Ali ibn Zahir!" But she spoke without enthusiasm. Clanton sensed that her relationship with Ahmed was a one-sided affair.

Without doubt he had taken her by force from some weak tribe far to the south or the east. There was still plenty of raiding and women-snatching going on in the desert, and he knew Shaykh Ali was a powerful chief who dwelt somewhere south of the Atlas Range. But he did not care. The nearness of this desert beauty, the feel of her lightly-veiled flesh under his fingers was making him drunk again, and with a wilder, more reckless intoxication than that of liquor.

He had forgotten Zoura; this girl had everything *she* had, and more; she was vibrant with that intangible quality some call glamour, which sets the natural artist apart from the willing worker, however skilled and lovely.

ALL his life Clanton had been following his impulses, and now there was no resisting the peremptory urge of his primitive nature. He saw in this girl's eyes the same light he knew burned more fiercely in his own, and that was enough.

"To hell with Ahmed!" In sudden savage hunger he crushed her to him, found her hot red lips, until she caught fire from his ardour and her arms locked in equal fierceness about his neck, as she gave him kiss for kiss. There was a profusion of silk pillows in one corner. She yielded meltingly in his arms as he lifted her from her feet and carried her across the tent. The soft white gleam of her flesh in the mellow light made his head swim. Then for a time, Time stood still in the little striped tent.

SOME time later the girl squirmed blissfully in Clanton's arms, stretched her white arms luxuriously above her head and then threw them about his thick neck, laughing with the pure joy of living. She kissed him with a gusto still not satiated in the slightest.

"I love you!" she sighed. "The first

man I ever loved! I hate Ahmed. He is cruel. He stole me by force. I am Aicha. What is your name, beloved?"

"I'm Wild Bill Clanton," he answered, running his fingers through her silky locks. Her dark eyes flared with sudden terror and the clasp of her arms was suddenly convulsive.

"You are the man Ahmed was to meet at dusk by the Well of Mansourah! To lead to your death!"

"What are you talkin' about?" he laughed. "He's Zouza's cousin, and—"

"He is not!" She was shaking him in a very frenzy of fright. "She betrayed you! Ahmed is Shaykh Ali's spy, and for Ali he laid a trap for you! Listen, I know all about it! There are no lions in Alloufa! Zouza lied about that, as about many things, according to Ahmed's instructions. He waits at Mansourah, not to guide you to Alloufa, but to take you captive to Ali, who has ridden up from the southern desert and lies with his tents not many miles from this spot.

"Ali sent Ahmed into Tebessa to draw you from the city by trickery. So Ahmed dogged your steps until he learned you were visiting Zouza—may she sit on hot coals! Then he gave her money to trick you as she did."

"But why does Ali want to capture me?" he demanded.

"Zulaykha, his wife, who rules him even as he rules his tribe, has turned from him and refused to grant him her favor until he brings you to her. She is the sister of Muhammad Pasha."

That seemed to suggest some kind of a connection with that cargo of rifles. Muhammad Pasha was a Turkish adventurer, playing a dangerous game for high stakes in Tripoli. Doubtless he needed guns.

"The moon has risen! Let us go,

quickly! There is a horse tied behind the tent which will carry us both. Ahmed may tire of waiting, and—"

EVEN as they stepped outside the tent door a group of riders swept over the ridge to the north and were upon them. Ahmed, weary of his long vigil at the Well, had returned. No time to run now.

From a heap of firewood Clanton snatched up a heavy fagot as the Arabs sprang from their horses and rushed at him. Oaths, shouts, the impact of blows rang to the sky. Ahmed, his face convulsed at the sight of Aicha cringing beside Clanton, forgot his command to take the *Roumi* alive, and lunged in, pistol thrust out at full arm's length, firing blindly. Clanton grabbed the long barrel and twisted it aside. As the powder burned his cheek he smashed his rude bludgeon down on the frantic Arab's head, and felt the bone give way. But even as he knew he had killed his man, a rifle stock splintered on his own head, and the lights went out.

Clanton recovered consciousness bound in a saddle, riding among his captors. The first streaks of dawn were lighting the eastern sky. Profanely he demanded to know where they were taking him, and what had become of Aicha.

"We take you to Shaykh Ali ibn Zahir," they answered, without resentment. "As for the girl, she sprang on a horse tied behind the tent, and fled away when we tried to seize her."

THE sun was up when they topped a low ridge and saw half a dozen tents before them.

Shaykh Ali ibn Zahir, a tall, stately man with a pointed black beard, and half a dozen wild-looking cut-throats behind

There she was, clad only in horn-rimmed spectacles, on a runaway donkey!

him, stood before the largest tent. He eyed Clanton murderously, but restrained his obvious anger and said quietly: "Your enemy, my wife, awaits you."

"I'm no enemy of hers," grunted Clanton. "I never saw her."

"Perhaps not. But you helped the Italians catch her young brother and send him to prison, she says. She has denied herself to me, until I brought you to her." He meditated for a moment, wry-

ly. "Never in the history of *Al-Islam*," quoth he, "has a *shaykh* led a *Roumi* in to his wife, and left them alone! Yet that is what she requires! What she means to do, I do not know. I know this: that she is safe from you, because your hands will be tied behind you, and my most faithful eunuch on guard over you. Who can fathom the whims of women? Her whim is to punish you, alone in her tent. Perhaps she will let you live, after certain alterations. But you must understand that I cannot.

"It is shame enough that I let her have her way in this thing. You understand that I cannot let you live after you have been in my wife's tent, whatever the reason."

"Sure," said Clanton sardonically. "I understand. A hell of a *shaykh* you are, lettin' your wife boss you around!"

But the white man knew that petticoat domination in the desert is much more common than Westerners generally realize; and if Zulaykha was anything like her brother, it was not suprising that she should dominate Shaykh Ali, who was not noted for any particular strength of character.

He was led to the tent and thrust through the door. The flap was closed behind him. A dark-haired, dark-eyed beauty, unveiled, lounged on a great pile of velvet cushions. Near the door stood a huge impassive Soudanese, like an image cut out of black basalt, with a scimitar in his hand and the butt of a Luger jutting from his girdle.

Clanton scowled at the woman, who was an olive-skinned Turkish Juno, plumper and darker than Aicha, with generous contours only partly veiled by her sheer *gandourah* and the silk vest beneath. Clanton knew very well what sort of punishment a masculine captive might expect at the hands of a Turkish woman, but he was too mad to be apprehensive.

"What the hell you mean by tellin' your husband that lie?" he demanded. "I never helped send any brother of yours to jail, and you know it."

"I had to give him some excuse," she answered calmly. "My husband is a sluggard, caring for nothing but women. He is but a pawn in the game my brother plays. I thought he was a man when I married him. I find he is a coward. Had

he known my real reason for wanting you he would never have brought me up from the south and captured you for me. Enough. My brother has learned you have a cargo of rifles to deliver to the Berbers. I want you to write a letter to your mate, telling him to deliver the rifles to my brother, at a spot on the coast I shall designate.

"I won't do it!" he snarled.

"There are ways of persuasion!" Her heavy lids drooped over her glittering eyes, and she looked dangerous and cruel enough for any torture or bloody mutilation. But Clanton was not impressed. He was as tough as he looked.

"Go on and shoot the works," he growled. "I'm a gone goose anyway. Those guns are goin' to friends of mine, not to your fat-bellied brother. They're patriots. He's a blasted thief! You can't hurt me bad enough to make me write that letter."

ZULAYKHA eyed him with more respect, recognizing in him a man who might be led by a woman, but who was not to be driven. She rose suddenly, came to him, untied his wrists and drew him toward the cushions.

"Let us be friends," she urged. "You could go far, with my brother and me. Never mind the black man. He is my servant—not Ali's. And he is faithful to me."

Clanton wondered just which one of them was mistaken about the negro. He understood her game, but he was a man who plucked fruit when he found it, and not even the realization that only a miracle could keep his severed head from rolling in the sand within the next hour could cool the customary ardor of his reckless blood. He was not one to let a woman do all the wooing. Zulaykha, preparing to vamp him with all her arts, found the game taken out of her hands as he drew her onto his lap without hesitation. Always adaptable, she yielded supplely.

"Ally yourself with me!" she whispered, throwing her round arms about his neck, and rubbing her full, velvety cheek against his. "Let Muhammad have the guns! I will make Ali spare your life!"

He knew she lied deliberately. Whatever her dominance of the Shaykh, she could never persuade him to spare a man she had taken into her tent, even though Ali suspected nothing of this love-making.

"Leave Ali and ride with me to Tebessa," he suggested, fighting for his life with every trick that occurred to him, even while he explored the perfumed recesses of her *gandourah* and the filmy vest beneath. "We'll sneak out the back side of the tent, grab horses and ride!"

"I cannot," she breathed, seizing his hand and drawing it to her. "Ali is a fool, but we need his tribe, Muhammad and I, and his money in our schemes. Write the letter for me! You shall have what I have refused Ali, and freedom and gold besides!"

He knew she lied. Once she got that letter, Ali could have his head. He pretended to be intoxicated by his passion, replying incoherently to her urgings as he sparred desperately for time and a plan of escape. And his head *was* beginning to swim a little; and Zulaykha's shudders of ecstasy were not all feigned, as his caresses grew more and more ardent. The black eunuch yawned, whether with indifference or to conceal envy, Clanton did not know. But he did know the moments of his life were fast slipping away. Zulaykha dexterously led him on, increasing her importunities.

He couldn't stall her off much longer.

Presently she'd realize his game, and turned from seduction to torture. Well, at least his hands were free, and he'd go down fighting.

OUTSIDE, suddenly, a voice shouted: "*Sidi!* A white woman! Riding alone, within a mile from camp!" It was a look-out on the ridge.

An instant clamor answered him, Ahmed's voice exultantly yelling orders. Zulaykha sat up on Clanton's knees, a little irritated.

"Listen at them! Ali shows decision and determination only in the matter of women! Hear them saddling and mounting? He could never resist the opportunity to chase a white woman."

"You mean he'll snatch her?" demanded Clanton incredulously.

"Why not?" she demanded impatiently. "Nobody will know. We'll be deep in the desert by nightfall. Ali is terrified by the thought of revolt and intrigue—that's why I deceived him about the rifles. But he'll risk his neck for a woman—especially a white woman."

"Well, he won't get away with this!" Clanton leaped to his feet, spilling Zulaykha in a sprawl of bare, olive-tinted legs and hips. She swore at him in Turkish, French, and Arabic.

"What do you care?" She herself felt no jealousy toward a chance-caught captive. "Let the fool do as he wishes with her. You and I—"

"To hell with that!" He sprang toward the door, as the drum of hoofs diminished in the distance. Zulaykha screamed: "Stop him!" The black swung with his scimitar. Clanton ducked and swung with his left. It connected. The black kissed the carpet, with a fractured jaw.

Clanton snatched the pistol from his
(Continued on page 126)

TEARS for

His lashing feet
knocked her from
the dock.

*Bill Erwin was tough; he could take plenty punishment.
And he had to do just that when he ran up against the most
passionately cruel woman in the criminal world*

BILL Erwin liked his job; it was
easy, he had no immediate bosses,
and it gave him plenty of spare
time. An easy berth for an ex-sailor.
The old warehouse and dock where he
presided as watchman might have been
lonely to many, but Bill was used to it.
Even Hogarth, the owner, never came
around and Bill often wondered at the
necessity of having a watchman. In-
surance, of course, was the answer.

Every evening Bill found time to
shoulder his way through the home-
comers until he made South Street.
Mike's place was his goal. Flat-faced
Mike whose dump was known all over
the world wherever sailors congregated.
Tonight, the air was chill and the squalid
little bar-room was cheerful. A row of
seamen, Swedes, Slavs, with a red-head-
ed Mick occasionally interspersed, lined
the rail.

RATS

By Cary Moran

"A shot," grinned Bill, "a shot of the usual."

Mike himself grunted, slid along the back of the bar.

Bill's eyes searched the mirror. He started. *His dame!* What the hell? A little rumble in Bill's thick throat showed his anger. Turning he caught Meg's eye. She winked.

NOW Meg was a member of the oldest profession in the world. When she winked, Bill knew something was afoot, and as Meg was his girl, knew that undoubtedly he would share in the net profits. The girl murmured something to her escort. The man immediately began to hammer on the table with a heavy beer stein. Mike shuffled around from behind the bar for the order, his beetling brows drawn together in the special frown reserved for drunken customers.

The man with Meg mumbled something, waved his arm expansively. Mike's scowl relaxed. Drinks for the house! Everyone at the bar turned to grin at the buyer, lifted their glasses in salute. Over the drunk's shoulder Meg winked again. Her companion saw the wink, turned to glower at Bill, saying something from the corner of his mouth to the protesting girl.

For a moment Bill could do nothing but stare open-mouthed at Meg's friend. The man's browned face was almost as fleshless as a death's head, his eyes so deeply set in the skull as to be almost invisible behind the high cheek bones. The mouth was a broad, sensual gash, more purple than red, and a great white scar running from temple to chin, dipping in suddenly to catch the upper lip, was like the welt of a cruel whip. For a moment the two men glared at each other and again Meg winked.

Bill reddened, turned back to his drink viciously. To he!l with her! If she wanted to play around with a damned foreigner, it was okay by him!

THROUGH the front door came three newcomers, two men and a woman. No table for these; they took a place beside Bill Erwin at the bar, the woman in the middle. Every eye in Mike's place was on the woman. Her companions were brown-skinned, roughly dressed, evidently sailors. She was slender, small, but curved sensuously. Her black dress spanned full hips like a caressing hand.

Bill grunted, dropped a coin to the sawdust on the floor. Stooping he caught a vision of a silken calf, well rounded, alluring. When he arose, he looked at her reflection in the glass and grinned.

She smiled. The man on her right glared at Bill, turned his back, and spoke to the woman in a crisp foreign tongue. She shrugged.

Another drink. And another. In the murky mirror Bill's gaze reverted to Meg. The man of the fleshless skull was half sprawled across the littered table. Meg was bending over him, her hands hidden from view. Evidently he had passed out.

Bill's neighbor-at-the-bar walked over to Meg's table. He spoke no word to Meg, but reached down and caught her companion by the hair. He looked into the drunken face, grunted with disgust, and pushed the head back down.

Meg said, "What the hell?"

The other brown-skinned man and the shapely woman walked to the table. The woman spoke to Meg. Meg flared a

reply, leaped to her feet. A brown hand shoved her down.

Bill sprang across the room. The long knife held so business-like by one of the sailors stopped him. The woman flashed him a smile.

"Don't get excited, my friend, this is a shipmate. We're taking him out."

Bill glowered, jerked his thumb at Meg. She pushed to his side haughtily, her nose in the air.

The two sailors got the scar-faced one on his feet. His legs were like rubber, his head wobbled uncertainly. The woman stepped close to him, slapped his face hard, hard enough to leave the print of her small fingers. The black, deepset eyes came open uncertainly. The drunk stiffened.

He said, "No, No! Damn you, no!" and struck at her with a clawing hand.

His long fingers caught and clung in the neck of her dress. A ripping, tearing noise—a pair of full, lemon-colored breasts suddenly half freed.

Her face whitened. For the space of five seconds she stood there oblivious of her trembling, swelling breasts, oblivious of everything but her insult. With the swiftness of a striking snake she jerked at her dress hem, revealed smooth chiffon topped by the warmth of flesh, the frill of dainty underthings. From her garter—glittering steel.

SHE almost had the man before her companions interceded. One held her arm, talked into her ear, quieted her, and finally she thrust the knife back into her stocking, pulled her torn dress together over her breasts and turned away. The two brown-skinned sailors, followed, the drunken man, now more nearly sober, between them. His feet seemed hardly to hit the floor.

At the doorway he turned his head.

His face was ghastly, his eyes wild and staring, but he made no sound. The door closed behind them.

A faint sigh from the crowd at the bar.

"Whee," said a squarehead, "I tank I like that dame!"

A guffaw. Kidding. Joking. Scenes of violence were not rare in Mike's place. Bill bought another drink and thought of pear-shaped breasts, soft flesh covered with smooth saffron skin, slender ankles, a gleaming thigh. What a woman!

Meg called him. He went to her table, sat down. "I'm going to scram, kid," she grinned. "Here." Beneath the table she thrust a roll of bills into his groping hand. Trust Meg! "He had quite a wad," she grimaced and I'm going to be long gone when they come back to see if he spent it."

She stood up, stopped for a moment to put a similar roll of bills into her stocking top. Bill stared at white flesh admiringly.

"I'm going down to the place," he said. "How about coming down there and laying low? We'll have some fun."

"Later," she said, and tossed a little red package on the table. "Take this too. The mug had it. Maybe you can play with them."

The red tissue package was a paper of Chinese firecrackers. Bill laughed, dropped them in his pocket, meaning to give them to one of the kids on South Street.

He turned up his coat collar and walked along thinking of the evening's occurrences. He grinned at the thought of Meg—trust Meg to come out ahead! —but licked his thick lips at the thought of the other woman in the saloon. Now, *there* was a dame!

He turned into the smelly alley he usually took, a short cut to the empty warehouse. The feeble flare of the street lamp far ahead was sickly in the thick fog. Halfway to the light he came on the rickety side gate of his own domain.

Ahead someone screamed. Bill froze. Again that scream, shrill, filled with fright, pregnant with pain! He made out a huddle of figures farther along, ran toward it. The figures, three of them, turned and ran at the approach of his hurrying footsteps. In the sickly glare of the arc-light he saw them. One was a woman.

One dark blotch remained in the alley at Bill's feet. He stooped quickly, lit a match, dropped it cursing. *The dead man was Meg's companion, the drunk in Mike's place!* His eyes bulged with horror, his nostrils were extended, his mouth gaped open. The blue tongue protruded from bluer lips. About his scrawny neck, almost completely concealed, a thin strand of wire, twisted tightly from behind.

The man's clothes were literally turned inside out. Bill sickened at the victim's tough luck. Evidently they were rolling a poor drunk who had already been taken! But why the wire? Why kill him?

HE ran down the alley in search of a policeman. A truck rumbled by. A sea-going tug tooted somewhere in the harbor. But there was no policeman in sight.

Back through the alley, past the corpse, to the lighted street at the other end. Thank God for Clancy, Clancy the cop!

Another five minutes, Bill scratching his head, Clancy speaking disdainfully.

"Aw, you're drunk. If he was dead, where is he now? Dead men can't walk away! And where's the blood?"

"Listen, Clancy, I know a stiff when

I see one! He was right here, I tell you, right here, with a strand of wire buried in his throat!"

Clancy looked about a little longer. "Well, kid, I'll make a report. But with no corpse there ain't no murder. You better lay off the liquor." He ambled majestically back down the alley, his flash playing on all dark corners which might conceal a body. At the street he looked back at Bill, made a derisive noise with his mouth and walked off.

Bill made the cubbyhole of the warehouse that once had been an office. Now it held a cot, a packing box topped by a broken mirror, and a few odds and ends of clothes. He dug out a bottle, took a stiff drink, and sat back to think. Fumbling in his pockets for a match he encountered the red firecrackers, tossed them on the packing box. Dead men that disappeared! He took another drink.

The clock said seven. Time for his first round.

THE dock itself was silent and deserted as usual. Its rotting timbers were dangerous; Bill walked carefully lighting the way with a flash. There was nothing or no one in sight. He came back through the ghastly warehouse. A rat ran across the beam of light. The waves lapping against the piling, the thick fog, the creaking timber beneath his feet. Back into his cubbyhole.

He turned on the feeble electric light, leaped back. Suspended by its neck in

Beneath the table she thrust

the far doorway was the body of the scar-faced man. Its brown skin gleamed in the lamplight, the corpse seemed to sway and dance in the breeze, the toes barely clearing the floor. The blue tongue seemed to protrude in derision at the frightened Bill.

"Pretty, isn't it?"

Bill whirled. The woman of Mike's place and her two Eurasian companions stood right behind him. She held a flat automatic in her hand. "Pretty, isn't it," she repeated and her black eyes glittered evilly. Slowly Bill raised his hands. One of the men walked to him, twisted his hands down behind his back, tied them with a piece of wire. The woman walked to him with a prance and surge of her hips, a thin smile on her mouth. He glimpsed a yellow mound of pointed flesh through the torn place of her dress.

Her hands slid in and out of Bill's clothes. His knife, his handkerchief, the keys, the flashlight. All were tossed on the cot. She found the roll of money Meg had given him; it followed the rest of the stuff. She ripped his shirt open, searched him thoroughly. Stepped away.

something into his hand.

MEG'S sobbing wakened him, pierced the black veil of his heavy sleep. Unbelieving, he looked about, saw the three bending over the cot he slept on.

"No," Meg was sobbing, "I don't know! I don't know, I tell you!"

One of the men leaned over her, clamped a brown hand roughly across her twisting mouth. It shut off her moans, but as he moved aside Bill saw Meg.

Her eyes were wild, protruding with horror above the brown hand. Clothes had been torn from her body. Her breasts swayed and trembled, crisscrossed with shallow wounds. The woman leaned over her victim, and Bill heard her gloating voice.

"Once more I ask. And then I try another method. What did you do with the package you got from the drunken Tami?"

The girl moaned, shook her head a little beneath the rough palm that held her.

Slowly, an inch at a time Bill worked himself to his feet. His hands were still bound behind his back, his mind still dizzy with the pain he had suffered. He saw the flash of the knife in the dark woman's hand, heard Meg's muffled moan of pain, saw the blood spurt in tiny drops from the shallow cut. He launched himself, feet foremost. *Crash.*.

They went down together, the torturess, the two seamen, and Bill. Hands tied securely Bill lashed out with both heels, roared aloud in pain and rage as

"She gave you a package, my friend. I want it."

"Who? Package? Why—"

The eyes narrowed a little. She stepped in quickly, hit him across the face with the automatic. Bill would fallen except for the man behind him. The woman's eyes glittered, she licked her lips, stared, fascinated, at the trickle of blood that swept down Bill's cehek.

"I like to do that," she said softly. "I want the package that woman gave you. I know you have it, she told us so."

Dumb Bill! What package? He shook his head, not from stubborness, but from stupidity. A brown arm shot around his throat from behind, pulled him back, back, back. There was no pity in the woman's face. She lashed out with a pointed toe, kicked him cruelly in the groin. Waves of nausea swept over Bill. The arm released him. As he lay curled in pain on the floor, she leaned over him again, crashed the gun against his skull.

"Bring in the girl," she said and those were the last words Bill heard. Unconsciousness relieved his pain.

his feet were clamped together, his ponderous body turned face downward. A hard toe pounded into his ribs, his hips, his thighs. The woman's voice.

"Wait," she said softly, "we mustn't kill him now!"

They pulled him to his feet, dazed, semi-conscious. The red mouth of the woman smiled at him. She lifted her dress to thrust the gleaming dagger balk into its sheath. There was something akin to admiration in her eyes. "Put him in another room," she said. "We'll wait for the other and finish the job all at once!"

They dragged him toward the door. Almost there. The sound of approaching feet. A gesture from the woman. They flung his tottering bulk behind the packing box. The door opened. Bill heard an exclamation of surprise, a word of dismay, then the woman's taunting voice.

"Good evening, my husband! This is a surprise, is it not?"

"Leone! You!"

Cautiously Bill maneuvered until he peered about the edge of the packing box. His eyes opened wide in amazement at the scene.

THE newcomer was his boss, Hogarth, owner of this warehouse, head of a huge importing company!

He stood with his hands raised in the air, the woman standing before him gun in hand. Her confederates stood on either side of the white man, both brown faces impassive.

"Aren't you glad to see me? Or did you think me safely dead in the jungle? Why don't you speak, why don't you answer?"

Hogarth's face was deadly white, his eyes dilated, his nostrils quivering. His staring eyes were fastened to the swaying corpse of the dead man hanging in the opposite doorway.

"Look, Hogarth, look well! Do you recognize your man?" She spurned the corpse, with a foot swung the cadaver so the hideous face was turned toward the cringing man.

"You sent him after me, Hogarth, don't deny it! And he did your work well except that I did not die! He stole the *Tears,* he brought them here! But I lived, Hogarth, I lived, and I followed. Always a step behind him, a half a day, two hours, until here we find him again. Before he died, Hogarth, he admitted the whole plot, but the *Tears* he did not have!"

Her voice settled to a purring, throbbing growl, like that of a cat. Her eyes glittered balefully. The two Eurasians held Hogarth's arms. Before him she paused. "Speak," she said, "before I cut your black heart out. You have the *Tears?*"

The man shook his head frantically; his eyes bulged. "No! No!" Shakily. "I came here to meet him, that is all. He called me on the phone, said he had them, that he would bring them to me here! But I did not know he had attacked you, that he had tried to murder you! Believe me, that was none of my doing, Leone! I swear it!"

The flat of her hand crushed the lie back into his throat. His guards held him firmly. He cowered before the enraged woman.

BEHIND his packing box Bill was beginning to work his add'ed brain. If this raging woman was Hogarth's wife he knew her, knew of her, at least. Estranged for years the woman still had dealings with her husband. She was a recognized authority on the Cambodian ruins, those ancient temples and palaces left by a mysterious people in the Malayan jungles.

Bill himself had heard tales of Leone Hogarth in Singapore years before. Rumor had it then that she was Eurasian, that Hogarth had married her in some Indo-China port. Now she sought through these ruins for collector's items, relics of a vanished race, and sold them to her husband. Bill knew this. But the *Tears?* What were the *Tears?*

"Don't lie to me," the woman raged. "You were the only one that knew I had them. I cabled you, Hogarth, told you what I had and asked for an offer. You asked me to wait for your man, to meet me there. Then this murderer, this thief in the night!" She spurned the corpse again. "Oh, I know, I know! I even know how he brought them into this country! In a package of firecrackers! But where are they now?"

"I haven't seen them! It's a lie! You're wrong! I didn't—" protested Hogarth.

The dead man swayed in the doorway. Meg groaned on the dirty cot. From behind the packing case Bill called out.

"Hey! Why didn't you say you were looking for firecrackers? It would have saved a lot of trouble!"

He swayed to his feet, even grinned a little at the fire-eyed woman.

"Jeeze, lady you just said a package, but if you'd have told me a package of firecrackers. Yeah, Meg got a little red package from this mug, but I—"

Her eyes widened in amazement. They helped him to the packing box bureau. But the package was gone!

"It was there, it was there! I tossed it there!" he babbled wildly, excitedly.

Then there was utter silence in the room. The woman, Leone, glared suspiciously at her helpers. They, in turn, glared back at her. Together the trio encompassed the trembling Hogarth, the still bound Meg, the surprised Bill.

"I tossed them there," he kept muttering, "right there!" The woman shrugged, drew her men aside and spoke in a whisper.

One of the men picked Meg from the cot, threw her over a shoulder like a sack of meal. He went to the swaying corpse, held it until his confederate cut it down. Then, both shoulders laden, he went toward the door. Hogarth followed, prodded ahead by the second Eurasian, next Bill, followed by Leone, who lighted the way with a flashlight.

Leaving she turned off the light in the cubbyhole.

STRAIGHT through the warehouse, the boards creaking beneath her feet. Out through the end door onto the old dock. A bleak tool house loomed beside them. The laden man grunted, his companion kicked open the door. Tami's body thudded to the planks, lay grotesquely where it had fallen, the purple tongue thick and round in the rays of the light. From a corner a pair of red rat eyes peered questioningly.

Hogarth cried out once, broke from his captor, and ran down the planking toward the warehouse. The woman turned, her gun spoke once. Hogarth screamed and sprawled on his face. A man trotted over after him, leaned above him. Shortly he picked him up, padded toward the deeper shadows. A soft splash. Hogarth was gone. The man rejoined them.

Another dark shelter. They paused. "Take her in there," spoke Leone bitterly. "You may have her! Do what you like with her!"

"And the man?"

"I'll take care of him. He's lying but I'll find out. Go on, you!"

Almost to the end of the roofed dock. The water through the gaping doorways was oily, scummy in the faint light. It lapped against the pilings with a faint hissing, a slap and a throb, monotonous, maddening.

"Here," said the lady grimly as they came to a tall stanchion. "Back up to that."

He backed up to it, realizing that something terrible was to follow. A thin piece of wire went through his bound wrists, secured him to the stanchion.

"Lady," his voice was choked. "you're making a mistake. What could poor Meg and me know about this thing? She rolled a drunk, that's all, and gave me part of the stuff. Why, I don't even know what your *Tears* are! Killing me won't get them back!"

She lit a cigarette, stared at him calmly over the glowing match. "Don't lie to me! You put them somewhere and I'm going to find out. The *Tears*, my friend, are what we call the *Tears of the Gods*. They're worth a fortune; you know it. But you'll never get a penny for them so you might as well tell me where you've concealed them."

"What do you want with them?" Vaguely Bill realized that he must stall for time. Something might happen, something *must* happen.

"I'm taking them back where they came from! To a temple ten thousand miles from here! Once I would have sold them, but now I take them back to the Gods who gave them! The Gods of Pain!"

Silence. Bill waited, wondering whether yelling would help. He knew in his heart the woman would kill him before his first scream echoed across the empty waterfront.

"I don't know where they are, lady, so help me! I threw the package of firecrackers on the packing box! That's all I know."

SHE waited for no more. She leaned quickly and her skirt ripped beneath her fingers. With the strips in her hand she walked behind him. In spite of his frantic twisting and turning she gagged him effectively. Then a thin wire materialized from somewhere passed about his forehead, pulled him back tightly against the tall stanchion. He winced as it bit into his forehead. Sweat poured forth. His eyes threatened to break from their sockets. Presently the pressure slackened. She spoke in his ear.

"Why pretend? You worked for Hogarth. He sent you and your woman to meet Tami. She got the *Tears* and gave them to you!"

He tried to shake his tortured head, couldn't move. She came around in front of him, stood peering up at him a little wonderingly.

"You are a fool," she said softly, "but you are a strong man. I do not like this as much as I thought."

Her hand slid across his matted chest, felt the huge biceps, the protruding shoulder muscles. Her hair was in his face, the smell of her in his nostrils. Something in her glittering eyes held him. Suddenly he realized that he *wanted* her to hurt him! *More than anything else he wanted her cruel hands to inflict pain on his huge body.*

She was very close to him. Soft breasts throbbed against his big chest. Round hips were warm against him. Her eyes were slots of fire; her hands were flames that explored his bulging muscles.

Suddenly she snatched the gag from his mouth, pressed her own lips passionately against his. He tensed, his body ached, his brain was numb.

"Give me the *Tears*," she whispered thickly. "We sail with the dawn, my friend, and I shall take you with me. You shall be a king, a man of might among my people."

Again lips hot on his—

He tensed, shot both feet into the air, kicked out. The added weight of his body on the wire that bound his head was almost unendurable. Blackness threatened to overwhelm him. He saw her sprawling figure trip over a pile of loose boards, seem to totter on the edge of the dock for seconds, then splash into the bay.

FOR a long while he fought for consciousness. Only dimly he saw the wet body emerge, death in her eye, every line of her lithe body outlined by the

"She'll talk!" screamed the woman. "If she don't, I'll—!"

clinging garment. Somehow in her struggle in the water she had torn it. He made out the outline of a breast, noted a gleaming thigh through a long rent as she catfooted toward him. The knife glittered in her hand.

"Dog," she said and raised it, but a restraining wrist was on her arm—one of her men.

"Do not kill him yet," murmured the man.

She spat at Bill, listened to the whispered words of her servant. Presently she nodded and stalked away, the dress clinging wetly to rounded hips. The man unbound Bill from the stanchion, led him down the pier, thrust him, still bound, into the blackness of a toolhouse and slammed the door.

Utter silence. The blackness was a cloak to blind his eyes. Then gradually he made out the *lap-lap-lap* of the waves beneath him. Something stirred in the darkness.

"Meg," he called softly, "Meg."

A groan. Silence.

Quietly he lay there, unable to get to his feet. Sweat was thick on his forehead. Suddenly all around him the patter of tiny feet, the swish of fetid furry bodies. Something c o l d, nauseous, against his face. He shook his head frantically. The f u r r y something squealed and pattered off. *Rats.* Dozens of them, hundreds of them, vermin infected, as large as small cats. His flesh crawled. A dozen times in the next ten minutes he imagined the feel of pointed teeth in his body.

He roared, unable to bear the agony.

"Bill! Bill! Are you here?" Meg in the same room!

"Over here," he directed. "Are you tied up?"

"No! I'm coming, Bill, I'm coming!"

A SHORT three minutes and he held her in his arms. Half naked, scarred and weak from fright she shivered against him, her arms about him.

"What a hell of a fuss over a package of firecrackers," she whimpered.

Bill kicked at a rat, then suddenly began to laugh.

Rats, that was it, rats!

"Baby, we've got to get out of here and back in my office! Firecrackers, you say? The dame told me they were worth a fortune! Jewels, maybe, Meg, diamonds! We'll be rich!"

She groaned. "And you know where they are!"

Again he roared with laughter. "Sure I do, baby, sure I do!"

The door was locked firmly. A few minutes prying at the window and it gave. Together they slipped out. Before leaving, Bill picked up a two foot length of rusty pipe that turned beneath his foot.

Tiptoe across the rotting planks. Blackness. There was no human sound but the noise of their own stentorian breathing. Through the warehouse itself, around piles of boards, into the black cubbyhole where Bill slept. Cautiously he lit a match.

"Careful," she whispered, "this joint would go up like a tinder box! Do you suppose they've gone?"

Bill was busy searching for a candle, afraid to risk the electric light. The girl continued.

"I think they've gone, Bill. I heard them talking about a boat beneath the pier and heard the noise of a motor just before I passed out. Maybe they got discouraged and beat it. They—"

"Look," Bill interrupted, pointing to a pair of shoes hanging on the wall. "The rats are so damned bad I can't even leave my shoes on the floor! Don't you see. I'll bet they carried off those crackers!"

The candle gave off a weird gleam. Shadows danced and flickered on the barren walls. Almost beside the door Bill found an enormous rat hole in the baseboard. Down on his knees, prying, pulling, tugging, sweating in the half light. It gave, squeaked shrilly as he pulled it loose.

"Good God!"

A rat's nest for truth. Pieces of oil soaked waste, scraps of burlap, paper, cordage, the accumulation of years of scavengering! A grey devil squeaked and ran into the blackness. With the pipe Bill had picked up, he pried through the debris. There in a far corner—*the innocent looking package of firecrackers.*

He handed them to the girl. The rats evidently had not cared for the taste of gunpowder, the firecrackers were scarcely touched.

"Open one," he said hoarsely. With nervous fingers she pried it open. Something rolled out onto the dirty floor.

"A pea," she said, "a black pea!"

"Like hell," grunted Bill jubilantly, "A black pearl! Twenty black pearls, the *Tears of the Gods!* I've heard about 'em! We're rich, kid, rich!"

"Twenty is incorrect!" A soft voice from the doorway. "Not twenty but forty! Give them to me, please."

"FOOL," the soft voice continued, "I knew you would lead us to them. I knew you lied, knew you had them."

"I didn't have them," Bill grinned a little ruefully, "the rats had them, not old Bill!"

As he drew erect he suddenly spun, threw the gaspipe into the center of the light beam. Before it hit the floor he fell on his face shoving Meg violently.

The automatic spat three times above his head as he tossed the red tissue package far back into the rat nest. He kicked the flaming candle after it.

Again the gun, a searing, stabbing, pain in his shoulder.

Bill fell on his back, lay there laughing like mad. "The *Tears of the Gods,* you've got them! You've got them."

A sheet of flame shot up the wall. The debris of years, oil soaked, combustible as tinder roared into heat. The woman Leone, her two helpers, fought at the base to get closer. To snatch the red package from the flames.

Someone dragged Bill away, out of the door, onto the coolness of the dock. Meg. He still roared with laughter. "Rats in a rat's nest!" he yelped. "Rats! Rats! Rats!"

The whole side of the building was aflame before they dropped off the edge of the dock. The thick water felt cool on Bill's wounded shoulder.

"Come on," gasped Meg, "let's swim for it. They'll be after us!"

Half choked with laughter and water Bill clung to the slimy piling. Off in the distance he heard a siren, knew a fireboat would be here shortly, saw the searching gleam of headlights pointed toward the deserted pier.

Overhead suddenly only a fast *spat-spat-spat!* Like a rapid fire gun.

"They're shooting at us," gasped Meg and tugged at him again. He laughed so hard he scarcely heard the patter of running feet on the planks above, the faint *putt-putt* of a motorboat at the end of the pier.

"That wasn't shots," he managed to gasp, "That was a fortune in pearls, two in each firecracker! A fortune in black pearls! They couldn't reach them! *The rats beat the rats!*"

They swam off into the shadows.

Diana Daw

By Clayton Maxwell

SHEIK TARAFI, OF ENGLISH PARENTAGE, WHO LOVES DIANA, HAS BEEN SORELY WOUNDED. THUS DIANA BECOMES LEADER OF THE ARAB BAND — SHE HAS JUST DEFEATED THE SHEBANS IN A PITCHED BATTLE

TED AND THE QUEEN OF SHEBA ARE CAPTURED ALONG WITH THE SURVIVING SHEBANS. UNAWARE THAT DIANA IS THEIR CONQUEROR, THEY ARE THROWN INTO PRISON IN TARAFI'S FORTIFIED CITY.

IT'S NO USE, RAMA — I CAN'T IMAGINE WHAT MADE ME BELIEVE I LOVED YOU — MY MIND SEEMS SUDDENLY CLEAR — I NEVER REALLY LOVED YOU — I WONDER WHAT HAS HAPPENED TO DIANA!

CURSE IT! THOSE LOVE POTIONS I GAVE HIM HAVE WORN OFF — AND NO WAY TO GIVE HIM MORE — UNLESS WE GET BACK TO SHEBA!

DIANA GOES DIRECTLY TO TARAFI'S ROOM

DARLING, — I FEARED YOU MIGHT DIE — IT IS WONDERFUL TO FIND YOU ALIVE! TELL ME THAT YOU WILL RECOVER!

LET ME CONGRATULATE YOU, DEAR, ON YOUR GREAT VICTORY OVER THE SHEBANS! NO — I'M FINISHED — MY ARAB PHYSICIAN TELLS ME THAT THE WOUNDS THEMSELVES ARE SLIGHT, BUT THE ARROWS WERE TIPPED WITH A DEADLY, UNKNOWN POISON —

SHEBAN ARROWS TIPPED WITH POISON! THAT QUEEN OF SHEBA KNEW PLENTY ABOUT DRUGS AND POISONS — I WONDER IF SHE KNOWS THE ANTIDOTES — I'LL HAVE TED MAKE HER TELL!

TED IS BROUGHT BEFORE DIANA

DIANA!

LEAVE ME ALONE WITH THE PRISONER — YES, DIANA — AND YOU'RE NOW MY SLAVE! YOUR FIRST TASK WILL BE TO PERSUADE THE LOVE OF YOUR HEART TO FIND AN ANTIDOTE FOR TARAFI, MY AFFIANCED HUSBAND — YOU MAY GO!

RAMA, THE QUEEN OF SHEBA, FED ME LOVE POTIONS — I WASN'T MYSELF — THE ONLY WAY I CAN PROVE I STILL CARE FOR YOU IS TO TRY AND MAKE YOU HAPPY — BRING YOUR LOVER BACK TO HEALTH!

SHE WHIPPED ME FOR A COWARD BEFORE THE LAST BATTLE — REVENGE WILL BE SWEET! TARAFI STILL LIVES — AND SHE IS IN THE ARMS OF ANOTHER — I'LL KILL HER AS AN UNFAITHFUL WIFE AND WIN TARAFI'S GRATITUDE!

I KNEW YOU WOULD HELP ME TED — KISS ME — JUST ONCE!

BELIEVE ME, DIANA, I NEVER LOVED RAMA

DEATH TO ALL TRAITORS!

52

THESE CHAINS ARE HEAVY!

TED--I--I HEARD HIS SKULL CRACK!

DIANA INTERVIEWS RAMA IN THE PRISON--

TED TELLS ME YOU KNOW AN ANTIDOTE THAT WILL CURE TARAFI. OUR POSITIONS ARE NOW REVERSED, RAMA. AS MY SLAVE I COMMAND YOU TO APPLY YOUR KNOWLEDGE AND RESTORE TARAFI'S HEALTH.

I KNOW THE ANTIDOTE--- BUT I WILL DO NOTHING TO HELP THE WOMAN WHO STOLE MY MATE, TED!

RAMA WOULD HAVE USED A HOT IRON!

FOR ONCE I'M GOING TO BE CRUEL -- A LIFE DEPENDS ON IT!

OH-H-H-H-H-H! I'LL--I'LL DO ANYTHING, DIANA!

IF HE DIES, RAMA -- SO DO YOU --- HORRIBLY!

I HAVE GIVEN HIM THE ANTIDOTE -- HE NEEDS REST --- LEAVE ME WITH HIM -- I KNOW WHAT TO DO FOR HIM!

YOU ARE THE HANDSOMEST MAN I HAVE EVER SEEN --- TAKE ME IN YOUR ARMS AND LOVE ME!

AND YOU HAVE THE MOST BEAUTIFUL FIGURE I'VE EVER SEEN, RAMA! THIS IS A FINE WAY TO TREAT A MAN WHO NEEDS REST AND QUIET! BUT I FEEL BETTER ALREADY!

THE ANTIDOTE WORKS QUICKLY, SWEETHEART!

THAT NIGHT RAMA STEPS OUT OF THE SICK ROOM TARAFI HAS FULLY RECOVERED --- AND -- HE HAS CHOSEN A NEW BRIDE --- ME!

MY LIFE WOULDN'T BE WORTH TWO CENTS IN THAT TOWN, TED, NOW THAT RAMA IS TARAFI'S FAVORITE! WE'D BETTER SCRAM!

NOR MINE! I CONKED HER OVER THE HEAD SO IT'LL BE SOME TIME BEFORE SHE COMES TO AND SPREADS THE ALARM!

ANOTHER EPISODE OF DIANA DAW IN THE JULY ISSUE OF SPICY ADVENTURE STORIES.

53

By LEW MERRILL

"This one's mine, comrades!" he shouted drunkenly. Then he saw Peter.

DEATH in the DESERT

He'd saved the life of the Arab chief's younger daughter and fallen in love at the same time. But it's the older daughter that the custom of the country bids him wed

UNDER the shadow of the mighty cliff of Jebel-Hauran, the blue-clad *légionnaires* of France now marched in a long column that wound in serpentine formation through the defiles. Behind them came the guns, behind the guns, the camel train, while mounted skirmishers deployed on either side.

Perpetual vigilance was needed against attack by the cruellest and most fanatical white barbarians on earth, the Druses of the Jebel-Hauran, whom France, in twenty years of ceaseless campaigning, had never been able to subdue. For them, death in battle meant immediate entrance into Paradise.

For miles on all sides the stony, sun-baked desert stretched away, until it yielded to the sweet waters, the almond, apricot, and orange groves of Damascus.

Peter Strange, time-expired *légionnaire,* walked in his place. In line with him were Novotsky, a huge Russian, Moller, a German, and Luigi, a Corsican. Strange had been longer in the Legion than any of them, his time was actually up when the detachment was sent from Algeria to quell the uprising in Syria. As soon as they reached Damascus, Peter would be entitled to his papers.

God, three days more, at most, and he would be free! In the pocket of his blue coat he had a letter, written eighteen months before by the girl in America, whose faithlessness had been the cause of that act of fatal folly. The old man she had married for his wealth had died a year later, and she was waiting for Peter, waiting till he could obtain his discharge.

Peter hadn't answered that, but there had come another, a year later. Her brother had been appointed Consul at Damascus, and she was going there with him. She'd be nearer Peter, in Algeria, and she was going to get Ralph to pull strings for his discharge ahead of his time.

Peter hadn't answered that letter either.

"ARRETE!" It was the noon halt. The long column came to a standstill. The weary *légionnaires* broke ranks and dropped upon the ground, munching their rations and eagerly awaiting the bottles of wine that were being brought up from the camel-train.

"And so the American receives his papers when we reach Damascus," grinned Luigi. "Cursed be the day when I enlisted, and I have still fifteen months to serve. Now if only we could see some real fighting, and have a few villages to sack—they say these women of the Druses wear gold necklaces and bracelets, all of them, besides being attractive little pieces."

"*Ja?*" muttered Moller. "I believe that when I see it. Give me the barracks life. These deserts of Syria are tenfold worse than those of Algeria, and the sun is just as hot. Besides, if there is any plunder, who gets it, the *légionnaire* or the *sous-officier?* As for the women, there are plenty of them everywhere."

"Still, the American will miss the chance of a battle," persisted Luigi. "They say these Druses are devils when they attack. They say, too, that we have been sent into this desert to act as a bait for them, while the flying column gets ready to attack their stronghold."

Peter said nothing. He was thinking of Maida Preston, and of the past. Could he be strong enough to forget her, after he was discharged?

"*Debout! Debout!*" was shouted harshly down the column. The crackle of musketry broke out upon the left flank, in the shadow of the mighty mountain. The skirmishers were retiring, firing from the saddle as they rode. And in the distance a cloud of white-robed horsemen were advancing at a gallop, and already their shouts were audible as a faint, thready sound that rolled along the base of the huge cliffs.

THE men were on the alert instantly, being formed into extended line by the sergeants and corporals. The guns were being unlimbered. Prone on the stony ground, Peter lay between Luigi and Novotsky, awaiting the attack. Behind them paced the officers, shouting directions:

"At three hundred meters, *mes petits!*

No firing till the order comes. Fix bayonets!"

There was a clicking sound as the triangular "Rosalies" slid into their sockets. The Druses were getting close now, their white mass almost blotted out by the cloud of red sand churned up by their horses' hoofs. Their yells were deafening, a prolonged, shrilling din caught up and re-echoed by the mountain walls.

"Fire!"

Repeating rifles roared, machine-guns belched a spray of leaden death into the thick of the desperate charge. The whole front of the mass dissolved. For a moment the attack semed to have failed.

But the pressure of those behind was irresistible, and, like a human river, the white-clad horsemen broke upon the line of the defenders, preceded by riderless horses, driven mad with pain and terror, that drove almost to the guns before they dropped, riddled with bullets.

The guns were opening now, but a machine-gun had jammed, the soldiers' magazines were empty, and now it was each man for himself, with his bayonet, against the white-clad fiends who sprang from their horses and advanced with gleaming scimitars.

Peter fought with the madness of the *légionnaire*, thrusting his bayonet fiercely into the whirling bodies that came rushing in upon him. In little knots the defenders were grouping themselves, thrusting, striking with clubbed rifles, in a din of devildom and a stench of dust and blood.

Perhaps that inferno lasted for two minutes, that seemed a century. Then the dust began to lift. Groups of Druses were sullenly retreating, disdaining to run, though the machine-gun bullets were mowing them down. A cluster of four still came desperately on against Peter's section.

"Ah, that's one for you, my friend!" shouted Luigi, as he ran his bayonet through a huge fellow with uplifted scimitar. He ran forward, Moller and Novotsky at his heels, drenched with blood.

Peter found himself confronting a young fellow a—boy, whose revolver snapped on an empty cartridge as he aimed it at him. For an instant he drew back his bayonet, then stretched out his hand.

"You're my prisoner," he shouted in French. And he saw that all the youth's companions lay dead about him.

"What's that?" shouted Moller, running up. "Prisoner? What do we want with prisoners?"

But Moller stopped, for under the white *abba's* sleeve he saw the gleam of a heavy gold bracelet.

Instantly the three men hurled Peter aside and flung themselves upon his captive. They tore away the white robe, disclosing two milk-white shoulders and two small, girlish breasts, the outlines of two slender hips revealed beneath a shimmering waist-cloth of finest silk. Two smooth legs showed bare beneath it, with white, rounded knees, and calves that were half-hidden by the boots of soft red leather.

"*Gott in himmel*, a girl!" gasped Moller.

THE *légionnaires*, with their own dead thrown into a supply cart, and their wounded carried in ambulances, or hobbling along beside them, resumed their march to join the flying column from Damascus in the cool of the evening.

Through the night they struggled on, in a territory that grew every mile more difficult. And all night, at intervals, Peter's three companions cursed the *sous-officier* who had forced them to relinquish the girl, and handed her over to the care of the transport officer, for conveyance to Damascus.

"*Gott,* I shall go mad!" raved Mo'ler. "White—white as you or I, American. Whiter than Luigi here! Such a body! such breasts! Those legs of hers! And a child, not more than eighteen at the most, and innocent, I'll swear to it!"

"Bah, wait till we reach Damascus," sneered Luigi, as he stumbled along, a bloody bandage around his head. "You'll forget her!"

Peter was thinking of the look of frightened appeal in the girl's eyes as he made that motion with his bayonet toward her. Did the Druses send girls to fight among their men? Those eyes of hers haunted him. For the first time in a long while he had ceased to think of Maida Preston.

It was not far from dawn when the weary column found itself trapped in another defile.

From the heights on either side volley after volley was poured into its ranks. From overhead huge rocks came tumbling down, crushing men's bones to fragments and stampeding the camel train. Guns were struck and knocked over, and in the darkness all attempts to form a fighting line were futile.

Retreat became a rout, and, as the *légionnaires* rushed back to seek shelter at the entrance of the defile, the yells of the Druses drowned the roar of vol'eying musketry, and an ambuscade leaped into life to cut down the bewildered fugitives.

Peter and his three companions had become separated in the dark. Peter found himself, when the first streaks of dawn were in the sky, wedged among some rocks with some dozen men from different troops, fighting for life against the hordes that surged around them.

Time and again the Druses got within closing distance of the little band, only to be repelled by bayonet charges. But already half the dozen were dead, the tumult of the retreat had died away, and the six, crouching among the stones, knew that daylight would witness their extermination.

It was growing light fast now. A morning mist, curling up the valley, hid everything beyond the rim of rocks behind which the defenders crouched. Then suddenly, out of that mist, there sounded again the furious Druse war-cry.

Something like an iron club struck Peter across the temple. He reeled, heard his own voice go from his lips in a wild cry, felt his nerveless hands drop the bayonet, and collapsed, inert, among the rocks.

LIFE? How could he be alive? It must be a dream, like the dream that Maida had been beside him, tending him, and pouring cool drinks down his parched throat.

Later he realized that he was lying on a bed in a room whose walls were of stone, with rugs upon the floor. Sometimes white-robed men would enter, stare at him in silence, and go out. Sometimes an elderly man with a kindly, wrinkled face beneath his turban, would enter, feel his pulse, make signs to him to protrude his tongue, and then withdraw, to enter into colloquy with some one outside in an unknown, uncouth language.

Peter knew now that he was a prisoner of the Druses, but why they had spared his life he couldn't know. And his bandaged head ached too badly for him to be able to ponder over this problem. Sometimes he thought he had relapses, and then he would drift into half-unconsciousness, in which again he fancied that Maida's hand was on his forehead.

He plunged down. The bayonet tore through chest and back.

Then one morning he awoke to full consciousness, to see a grave-faced, gray-bearded man standing beside him, looking at him with close scrutiny.

"Welcome, my friend," he said in Arabic. "I rejoice that you are at last out of the shadow of death, for assuredly you were at times well within that shadow. I am Abd-el-Rahman, the chief of my people."

"And my comrades?" asked Peter weakly.

Abd-el-Rahman was silent for a while. "Rejoice, rather, that you are alive, my friend," he said. "When you are well, you shall know the answer to your question."

Surely that dream of Maida had been nothing but a dream, for, except for the *hakim,* the native doctor, Peter's sole attendants were two young boys, who brought him his meals and looked after his needs, until the day came when Peter was able to get out of bed and stand on his feet.

They had taken away his uniform, and brought him the robes of a Druse, the boots and short trousers, the woolen undergarment, and the flowing *abba,* with its hood. Thus attired, Peter walked weakly out into the sunlight.

He found himself in the single street of a village, enclosed on all sides by mountain walls. There were few men there, but women peered at him out of doorways, and children strutted, naked as when they were born, and unconcerned by his appearance, up and down between the stone houses.

Peter walked a few steps, turned, and saw Abd-el-Rahman standing in the doorway of his house. The grim old chief was smiling.

"Come, my son," he said, holding out his hand, as if to a small child.

AND Peter followed him, not into the room he occupied, but into a long stone hall, with a curtain across one end. Here, on divans, were seated a dozen men, apparently, from their years, the elders of the village, and four young ones, who eyed Peter in surly disapproval.

"Sit beside me," said Abd-el-Rahman. "Your life was spared because you spared the life of my beloved child, Koraida, when she ran away to follow my eldest son, her brother, to the battle in which he died. Therefore, according to our custom, I pledge you my daughter's hand in marriage, and offer you blood brothership in our nation. And, if that does not please you, you are free to depart.

"Come, my son, and see your bride, in accordance with our custom," he added, rising and taking Peter by the hand.

He spoke a few words, and the rest of the men salaamed and departed. There sounded the scampering of feet behind the curtain, and then Peter stood beside the old chief in a dimly lit room, with divans along the stone walls, and rugs underfoot.

In the center of the room a veiled figure was standing like a statue. Abd-el-Rahman spoke softly, and slowly the draperies were swept aside, and the half-nude form of a girl appeared. Then, weak though he was, Peter felt his heart beat faster as he looked upon an almost flawless form.

Full, rounded breasts, pointing toward each armpit, a waist that seemed made only for the embrace of a man's arms, widening into a woman's hips, and the flawless legs that ended in two tiny feet firm planted upon the rug. Yes, Peter had forgotten Maida. For he knew this was the Maida who had tended him when he lay unconscious.

Abd-el-Rahman strolled nonchalantly around his daughter, as if he were exhibiting some prize animal, pointing out her beauties in full-flavored Arabic that brought the blood to Peter's cheeks.

And all this while he had not dared look up. Now, venturing to raise his eyes to the shapely head, with its coiled up masses of black hair, and the eyes, alight with tenderness in which lurked no mock modesty, he was suddenly appalled.

This wasn't his captive of the battlefield!

A S if reading his mind, Abd-el-Rahman said: "This is my elder daughter, Fatima. My daughter, Koraida, whose life you spared, and whom the chance of war mercifully restored to me, is her younger sister.

"Choose, now, my son, for I know that the claims of your own land must be strong, and there is likely to be a struggle in your heart. Yet, if you join us, my child will not shame you, for both my daughters were taught at the French school in Damascus before we Druses decided to abandon all commerce with the invaders. If you wish, you may delay your decision for a while, but not again can you see Fatima, until the nuptial ceremony."

Peter understood now. It was like the biblical story of Leah and Rachel. The elder daughter must be married before the younger, or she would be put to shame.

And a sudden gust of anger shook him. "I do not wish to seem ungratful," he said, "but the claims of my own land are stronger even than this maiden."

Abd-el-Rahman stroked his gray beard gravely and repeated Peter's words in the Druse language. The result was not what he might have imagined.

For Fatima suddenly became a screaming fury, and sprang at Peter, hands outstretched, clawing at his face.

Peter caught her by the wrists and forced her back. Suddenly she collapsed upon the floor in an agony of sobbing. From an adjoining room came the excited chatter of women.

"It is well, my son," said the chief, leading the way back behind the curtain. "I do not blame you, and, as for my daughter, let not yourself be distressed by a woman's tears, since it was evidently the will of Allah that this thing should come about."

T HE old madness for Maida had come back to him that night as he tossed on his bed. Fool, to have forgotten her because he had looked upon Koraida! Was his constancy any better than hers?

When he reached Damascus, if she was still there, he would obtain his discharge, and then go to her, marry her, and take her home to America.

The humiliation of that strange scene in Abd-el-Rahman's harem was still strong in him. It was far into the night before he dozed, still living through it again in dreams.

Then suddenly he was wide awake, with the consciousness that he was not alone. Something was crouching at his feet by the low bed, and sobbing, sobbing.

Peter sat up. If this was a trap, to make him take Fatima—well, he'd show them!

But this wasn't Fatima. This was Koraida, on her knees before him, her lovely face tear-stained and woebegone, in the faint starlight that came through the narrow window.

"My lord—thou goest in the morning,

and I love thee and shall never see thee again !"

She was in his arms now, and Peter hugged her close, held her fast. She nestled up against him like a child, and gradually her sobs decreased, while he tried clumsily to comfort her.

"I am shamel·ss. If they know, they will stone me to death," she whispered in French. "Thou thinkest me shameless, like one of the women of the bazaars, yes?"

"No," answered Peter. "No," he groaned. "I love you."

And it was as if Maida and Koraida were each tearing at his heartstrings. Can a man love two women at once? Peter did.

Yet, deep down within him, he knew that Maida was faithless. She had betrayed him for the sake of the rich old man, Cyrus Preston, the millionaire. Then he struck out his decision, as the flint strikes fire from steel.

"Come away with me, Koraida. Marry me!"

"My lord, it cannot be. It would shame my sister and my father and brothers. They would overtake us before we had gone ten miles."

He could not move her from that decision. And Peter let the matter slide. How could he plan rationally, when he held the warm living body of Koraida in his arms?

His hands were drawing her always closer, and her hands fluttered against his, in weakening protest; and then of a sudden she herself had flung herself against him ardently, and drawn his face down into the fragrant hollow of her throat. Then she raised his head, and her lips were fastened upon his with an abandon of passion that made Peter quite forget.

Peter fell back, appalled at the girl's jealous fury.

What did the future matter when he held Koraida's clinging, throbbing body in his arms, when they two seemed to merge into one being, and then drift off together into a blissful dream?

LONG later Koraida withdrew herself from Peter gently. "Lord, I must go." she whispered. "I shall love thee always. But we may never meet again."

He stretched out his arms toward her in the darkness, but she had flitted from him like a shadow, and he was alone.

Peter knew then that he must see Maida Preston in order to orientate himself. Then, when he was sure, he would return, and neither hell nor all the power of the Druses should keep him from Koraida.

Clad in Druse attire—for Abd-el-Rahman had told Peter that his uniform had been destroyed—and mounted on a swift black horse, he rode across the desert. Under his burnoose he had a loaded army automatic, the gift of the old chief, but he had declined the purse of gold that Abd-el-Rahman had tried to thrust upon him.

"If it be Allah's will," said the old man sadly, "perchance you will return, my son. Fatima loves you, and she is yours by the law of the Druses. God keep you!"

Now Peter was nearing Damascus, passing through the groves of dates and apricots. The road was blocked with crowds of Bedawi and farmers, seeking refuge in the city, driving their sheep and camels. Occasionally a patrol of *légionnaires* passed, but, evidently taking him for one of the Druses who were coming in to make submission, they did not stop him. So he rode up the Derb el-Mistakim, the oldest street in the world, moving foot by foot through a jostling crowd toward army headquarters.

The demeanor of the crowd was sullen and menacing. It was clear that the French military occupation was looked upon with no great favor. And several times Peter was halted by enthusiastic Nationalists, who caught at his bridle, and cried encouragement to him.

Peter fastened his horse at the end of a line of army horses near the headquarters building, and went on afoot. The great hall of the old Palace was filled with a waiting crowd, among whom French soldiers passed and repassed ceaselessly. At the further end, the entrance to the general's headquarters was guarded by a dozen *légionnaires*, with bandoliers and loaded rifles, who scrutinized each person carefully before he was admitted.

A man and a woman came out of the room behind. The man stopped, hesitated, and turned back for a moment, as if he had forgotten something, but the woman walked forward, as if unconscious of the staring throng. Both were Americans. The woman was dressed as Peter hadn't seen any woman dressed since he had left Algiers. She wore that Paris frock as if she was at a Westchester week-end party, despite the looks directed at her bare neck and silk stockinged legs.

Peter was face to face with her before they recognized each other.

Maida, with her fair hair, her large, candid eyes, her graceful figure! God, how the past came back to him. He tried to speak and could not.

"PETER!" they had moved apart from the throng. "Oh, Peter, they told my brother you had been killed in battle!" Maida's lips were tremulous. "He was inquiring for you, for the sake of old times. What are you doing, dressed like that? No, never mind! I'm so glad you're alive. We're at the Consu-late. You must come there as soon as you can. I'm Mrs. Gary now, you know. Mr. Gary's the manager of the oil line.

"Don't look at me like that! I wrote you, and I never heard from you. Did you expect me to wait for you for ever? We were married this Spring. Oh, Peter, I've so much to tell you. It's been so wretched. No more old men for me. I'm going back to America to get a divorce, and I'll be waiting for you, Peter. I'm going to make him pay through the nose for what he's done to me."

"You—needn't wait—on my account." Peter's blood seemed to have turned to ice. Now at last he saw Maida as she was, as she had always been.

"What do you mean, Peter? I've always wanted you. I want you now. I— we don't have to wait till I get my divorce," she added in a low whisper.

"Please go now," said Peter quietly. "I don't want to see you or speak to you again."

"What? You dare say that to me?" Maida's eyes flashed hatred, and she struck him hard across the face.

Instantly the two were surrounded by an excited throng. And into their midst three *légionnaires* came running. Peter saw himself looking into the face of Moller.

"*Gott in himmel! Gott!* It is you, then, you damned deserter, who hid among the Druses after betraying us. We knew there was a spy. *Gott*, so many dead, and you—you dare come here like that. A spy, comrades! Arrest him!" he shouted.

But the hall was in a turmoil. Jabbering Arabs and Syrians had clustered about Peter, hurling themselves upon the soldiers; fists were whirling and rifle butts were crashing. Turmoil became riot. Peter saw Maida dragged to safety by one of the *légionnaires*. Then he was being forced toward the entrance in the thick of the jam, while the French soldiers yelled and shrieked at him impotently behind it.

Peter, forced down the steps and into the street, where an excited crowd was already milling, suddenly laughed. He was through. He had served his time, and he was through. He was going back to Koriada.

In a moment he was lost amid the crowd of Druses, Arabs, Syrians, Marionites and Bedawi, all the motley races in robes like his, that jostled and scrambled, and shrieked invective against the French. With difficulty he made his way to the place where he had left his horse.

But all the horses were gone.

Peter laughed again as he made his way toward the Roman gate through which he had entered.

IT was nightfall before he was free of the fruit groves, and saw the dun of the stony desert stretching away before him. Far in the distance Peter could see the huge cliffs of Jebel-Hauran. All through the night he walked, and at the first signs of dawn he dropped behind a rock and snatched an hour of sleep.

He was awakened by the blazing sun. Damascus was no longer visible behind him, and the mighty cliff seemed hardly nearer. Peter struggled to his feet and plodded on.

There was no sign of life on the vast desert. The sun became a furnace, drawing out every drop of moisture in his body, parching his throat until his swollen tongue protruded like a dog's. But doggedly Peter kept his face turned toward the huge cliff, standing out like a wedge upon the desert's face. All through the day, stumbling over the débris of stones, scuffing up the sand with the toes of his scorching boots,

falling sometimes from utter weariness, and again rising and moving on.

Slowly the huge red orb of the sun moved across the sky. It dipped into the west, it sank, and in an hour the icy cold of the desert night replaced the furnace of the day. Peter pulled himself together now. All through the day he had been conscious of a division in his personality; the watching part of him, with its memories, and the automaton that it guided, pulled to its feet when it faltered, and kept pointed toward the Hauran. Now Peter was himself again, despite his raging thirst, and the cliff was nearer, a dark wedge in the dark curtain of the night.

Still, that night's march was the triumph of mind over brute matter, and only the legs of a *légionnaire* could have accomplished it. Peter fought thirst and fatigue, as if they were twin monsters, and at last, when the wind of dawn was in the air, he found himself not far from the mountains.

Then suddenly there came to his ears the distant roar of rifles, a faint, confused din like an undertone. Above the mountains appeared a slender spire of fire.

But he was among the rocks at the mountain's base now. Crouching there, when dawn broke, he saw a column of *légionnaires* moving away from the cliffs in the direction of Damascus.

Suddenly his heart was filled with apprehension. Was this the flying column that had been expected to unite with his own regiment? Had they stormed Abd-el-Rahman's stronghold? Then what of Koraida?

HE began scrambling madly up the rocks, until he came upon a goat track that ran up toward the mighty summit. He knew where he was, as soon as the sun rose. This was the path by which

(Continued on page 116)

"You think I am beautiful," she murmured.

EEL

I LIKE the name—The Eel. They've been calling me that ever since I began working on the theory, years ago, that the world owed me a living and damned if I wouldn't collect it. Matter of fact, the gentry of the law who tagged that name onto me like it a whole lot less than I do! Eels are slippery.

When Fournier sent for me I was in the Malay Straits, enjoying life with a dark-eyed, glamorous little English girl while resting up from a triumphant

tussel with the police of that ancient and venerable city, Bangkok. Fournier, having more eyes and ears than a colony of lizards, smelled me out and sent a message by one of his half-breed rats. The message said: "I can use you. Come to Singapore."

So I said to my glamorous little English girl: "Darling, either I sit here with you and go broke pouring liquor down your pretty throat, or I go to Singapore and do a job for this louse Fournier and make much money. Which is it?"

"You stay here," she sighed. "You stay and marry me!"

66

TRAP By JUSTIN CASE

The girl begs him to smuggle her to Sumatra, and it's the Eel's job to deliver stolen silks to the same place. But in the East, it's sometimes dangerous to mix pleasure with business . . . .

SO two days later I descended from the train in Singapore and wandered down through the native quarter to visit my old friend Lin Tsi. That English girl had too many ideas.

Understand, please, that I didn't slink into Singapore with my handsome face concealed behind false whiskers or spectacles. Not at all. Why the hell should I? The Singapore police wanted me, of course, same as the police in a dozen other cities in the Orient. They'd have given their collective right arms—willingly, too—for the privilege of walking me right off the end of the Malay Peninsula and dumping me in the China Sea.

But you can't jail a man until you get him with the goods.

As I was saying, I went ambling through the native quarter to visit the shop of Lin Tsi, who is a friend of mine, and who should I walk into but another old friend, Mr. Edmund Welch, who is

the ruling right fist of the local constabulary?

"So—The Eel is back!" he said unpleasantly, glaring at me. Then he snarled: "Listen, Eel. You'll make a mistake one of these days. Just a little mistake. Be careful you don't make it in Singapore. I'll be watching you, Eel—every move you make!"

"If you figure on following me around," I said, tapping him lightly on the stomach, "you will need to go on a diet of jumping beans, corporal." But to myself I thought, as I went on my way again: "It will behoove me to be very careful in this town. Apparently I am not liked by the locals."

Well, I was sitting in Lin Tsi's shop that evening talking to Lin Tsi himself, who is a very old and wise Chinaman for whom I have done many favors, and while I was sitting there enjoying the aromas of birds-nest soup and beche-de-mer from the kitchen out back, I was amazed to see a very gorgeous young lady entering by way of the front door.

This young lady had evidently never been inside Lin Tsi's shop before, for she stood looking around her in much bewilderment as if wondering what to do now that she had reached her destination. The shop was dark, and when Lin Tsi got up and shuffled toward this young lady, she gave a little start and said: "Oh!" Then she said, "I'm looking for a person called The Eel."

Lin Tsi, being cautious, wrinkled his parchment face into a scowl and murmured: "The Eel, madam? I do not think—" But I didn't give him time to finish. The young lady was very good-looking, and I had not had the pleasure of meeting a good-looking lady in quite some time.

"I am The Eel," I said.

"I—I must see you alone," she answered.

So I took her upstairs to the very private suite of rooms which, when in Singapore, I always rent from my friend Lin Tsi. And then, with the door closed against intrusion and a pair of ornate oil-lamps casting their yellow shadows upon the two of us, I sat and talked with the lady.

HER name, she said, was Mrs. Roger Smythe, which is a very pleasant-sounding name even in Singapore. And I am especially fond of sleek black dresses which reveal the contour of a woman's breasts and the exciting curves of her hips. Indeed I am.

"I need help," she said anxiously. "That is why I came here."

"You are in trouble?"

"Yes, yes, I am in trouble! I *must* get to Selatpandjang without my husband's knowledge."

Now Selatpandjang is a town on the northeast coast of Sumatra, across the Strait of Malacca. It is not far from Singapore but it is far enough to be inconvenient. "I am sorry, Mrs. Smythe," I said, "but I am here on business."

"I *must* get to Selatpandjang!" she insisted.

Well, I am at all times a human being, and this Mrs. Smythe was most attractive to me. Especially was she attractive the way she was sitting there in the dim light cast by two ornate oil-lamps. A woman as beautiful as she must have an interesting past, I thought; and perhaps, by exercising a certain amount of discretion, I could make her future very interesting also.

"Why," I said, "if I am not being too personal about this, must you go to Selatpandjang? A woman of your beauty, Mrs. Symthe, will find that uncouth town a dangerous place to abide in, I assure you."

"You think—I am beautiful?" she murmured. "Then you will do what I ask of you?"

"I am sorry, Mrs. Smythe, but it will be impossible."

"Nothing is impossible," she said, smiling gently upon me as she allowed her sinuous body to slide back upon the divan. "If money does not interest you, perhaps we can arrange other compensations . . . "

"Yes?" I said, raising my eyebrows.

"Compensations," she murmured, "in advance."

Now I am every inch of me a gentleman, despite the names which the police of various cities have bestowed upon me. It being apparent to me that Mrs. Smythe was sorely in need of assistance in one form or another, I allowed my thoughts to run as follows:

"Perhaps," I thought, "the little job

I am to do for Fournier will enable me, without much trouble, to transport this Mrs. Smythe to Selatpandjang. As a matter of fact," I thought, "it would be most scurvy of me not to take Mrs. Smythe to Selatpandjang. The lady is very lovely, and the compensation she offers—in advance—is apt to be very interesting indeed."

As I have said before, there were two ornate oil lamps in this little apartment of mine. When I pulled one of these lamps toward me and turned the wick down until the lamp exuded merely a pale yellow glow, the lady on the divan said very softly, "That is so much better," and smiled at me.

When I had turned the other lamp down the same way, the lady said very softly indeed, "Do you mind? It's rather warm in here . . ." And then, still smiling, she fumbled with buckles and buttons and whatnot, and gracefully slid the sleek black gown up over her head and draped the gown over the back of a chair.

Well, I had not noticed it was warm in the room before, but I realized now that it was warm indeed. In fact, I had not gazed at Mrs. Smythe more than a few minutes before the blood within my body had begun to move around in a most heated manner, creating strange sensations inside me.

I was acquainted, of course, with the fact that women in Singapore were in the habit of wearing few articles of clothing, because in that part of the world clothes are apt to become hot and sticky and most uncomfortable; but the few bits of transparent material now clinging to Mrs. Smythe's lucious body were practically of no account whatever. In fact, the lady was—in that dim lamp-light—so nearly nude and so voluptuous-

ly lovely that I found myself staring at her and holding my breath.

"Well?" she said softly.

"You are practically in Selatpandjang right now," I said.

She laughed, and moved over to make room for me on the divan, and in a moment more I was sitting there with the lady's back warm and heavy across my knees, while my left arm curled nicely under her neck, allowing her head to tip back so that her eager red lips hung alluringly beneath my own as I bent my head forward.

THERE are many ways of kissing a woman. Having been around a bit, I know most of them, but this Mrs. Smythe had been around also, and I would say in strange places. The heat of her pulsating lips, which remained parted, crept slowly into my own body and then was driven violently through every separate inch of me.

That kiss lasted a long time. While it was going on, my arms couldn't stay in one place, and they scraped dainty bits of gossamer, as they deliriously hugged undulating soft flesh.

I discovered then that this Mrs. Smythe was very human after all, for in a few minutes she began breathing hard and squirming against me in an effort to get closer. The warm flesh against me began to tremble.

"If this lady learned these things in Selatpandjang," I thought, "Selatpandjang must indeed be an interesting place."

Then the lady said in low whisper: "Don't you think it would be cozier here without lights?"

I was sleepy when I stood up later, to light the lights again, and when I turned back to the divan after so doing,

Mrs. Smythe was smoothing the tiny bits of silk about her lovely person.

"You have strong hands," she said. "Look." And I saw that my fingers had at one time or another made a trio of reddish marks on one of her exquisite shoulders.

Then she said: "You will take me to Selatpandjang?"

And I said: "If you will come here tomorrow night, about midnight, you will be in Selatpandjang before the following morning."

SOME time later that evening, while I was enjoying the luxury of a cool bath, Lin Tsi knocked on the door of my little apartment. Being a very patient man, he knocked several times, and then, when I shouted to him that my modesty would not permit me to come parading from the bathroom at that moment, he answered that a young lady had called to speak with me upon matters very urgent.

"She is from Paul Fournier," Lin Tsi said. "And," he said, "she is exceedingly attractive."

The girl was indeed easy to look upon. Not more than twenty years old at the most, she had a wealth of dark wavy hair and possessed two slumbrous dark eyes in a face far prettier than the average. She said her name was Regine, which is French, and she said also: "I work for Mr. Fournier." And she did not seem to be at all shocked by the vivid yellow-and-black dressing-gown in which I had wrapped myself.

"It is indeed a pleasure to know you, Regine," I said.

She smiled and sat down, and, by the light of the ornate lamp beside her, I saw that she was exquisitely proportioned. When I suggested, however, that a gin sling would be most refreshing on so warm a night, she shook her head in negative reply and said: "I am here on business. Mr. Fournier sent me with this." And she handed me a slip of paper.

The message, which was from Fournier, read briefly: "In the name of God, why are you so slow in coming to visit me? Come at once! The bearer of this note will escort you to my new headquarters."

"You have read this?" I asked Regine.

"No," she said sweetly.

"Read it then, while I am getting dressed."

I did not close the bedroom door while I was dressing. In my profession, it is best always to know everything that is going on—and one cannot see through closed doors. Yet this little girl was so light on her feet that I did not hear her come to the threshold; and, being busy at that moment before the drawer of a bureau, where I was pondering a choice of shirts I did not know that the young lady was watching me until she said sweetly, from the doorway: "So you are The Eel. I have always wondered what The Eel looked like."

I turned and stared at her "Madam," I said, scowling, "this is indeed embarrassing!"

"But I am not embarrassed at all," she protested. "I think you are very handsome."

Well, I have definite aversions to being gazed upon by young ladies while I am only two-thirds dressed. I made haste, therefore, to finish clothing myself. At the same time it was most apparent that this Regine person was either very innocent or very, very sophisticated, and I said to myself: "Eel—

we shall one day find out a great deal more about this girl."

There was, however, no time for that now, since Fournier was undoubtedly fretting and fuming over my delay in presenting myself. I said to Regine:

"It was necessary," Regine shrugged. "The police were learning too much about him."

"You mean—he is now in hiding?"

"I swam aboard," she said calmly. "I'm going with you!"

"Are you ready?" And then, together, we went out into the streets.

THERE are sections of Singapore where tourists and other thrill-seeking persons seldom intrude. Tourists would perhaps be unsafe there from slinking creatures who would at all times commit murder or mayhem for the contents of a victim's purse. Yet it was into one of these sections, close to the waterfront where a stink of fish and bad fruit hung heavy in the air, that my amazing guide led me.

"Fournier, I see, has changed his address," I murmured.

"No. He is merely more cautious."

We came at last to an unsavory doorway to the left of a fish market; and after leading me up a flight of dark stairs and along a corridor where I freely cursed the gloom on all sides of me, my guide knocked thrice upon a door, and the door was opened by Fournier himself.

"So," he said, ignoring my companion and gazing straight at me, "you have come at last."

I was indeed surprised to see the elaborateness of the fellow's new home. This, I had suspected, was merely a temporary hiding-place from the police;

but I was mistaken indeed. Rich furnishings met my wandering gaze, and it was obvious that Paul Fournier had established himself in all his glory, contemptuously disregarding the squalor of the slums around him.

We sat together at a small table and we were quite alone, for Regine had vanished like a shadow. When I had consumed a drink, Paul Fournier leaned toward me and said very softly: "Now listen, Eel."

"I am all attention," I said, smiling.

That was no lie, either, for a man would be foolish indeed not to be all attention while in the presence of this Paul Fournier. I can name three men, without thinking very hard, who became careless in the presence of Fournier and were soon after transported, late at night, to a spot approximately one and one-half miles out upon the China Sea, where they were dumped overboard from a motorboat.

Paul Fournier is a large, uncouth person who permits nothing whatever to stand in the way of his greed. Moreover, he had sent for me upon this occasion because he needed me—not because he liked me.

"It is a very easy job I have for you this time, Eel," he said. "The payment is five hundred dollars in advance and five hundred more when you bring me a signed receipt from the consignee in Selatpandjang."

The intensity of my attention increased abruptly. "Where?" I said.

"Selatpandjang."

"That is indeed a coincidence," I thought. Aloud I said: "And the nature of this simple enterprise, Fournier?"

"Silks."

"Ah! Silks this time, not guns!"

"Three weeks ago," Fournier said smiling, "a merchant vessel in the South China Sea was raided by pirates, who looted the ship of a very satisfactory haul of silks. The loot is now stored in a waterfront warehouse here in Singapore and will be paid for handsomely when it is delivered to a gentleman in Selatpandjang. A motor launch will do the trick, Eel."

Very quietly he counted out five hundred dollars in bills and put the bills into my left hand. "The time," he said, "had better be tomorrow night. You will find the silks waiting for you at the old Webly warehouse. Take them to Mr. Jason Agnew in Selatpandjang and get a receipt. When you have delivered the signed receipt to me, you will get five hundred dollars more."

Then he said, scowling: "Be very careful, Eel. The local police have been searching for this load of loot ever since the merchant vessel was raided. Mr. Edmund Welch—you are acquainted with him, I believe—would give his eye-teeth to get his hands on the stuff."

"I shall indeed be careful," I murmured.

"For the sake of your own health, you had better be. Now," he said, "get out of here. Go out the back way, so you won't be seen."

IT was necessary for me to walk through two nicely furnished rooms on my way to the rear entrance, and, because I was unfamiliar with the place, I was confused by the number of doors confronting me. Not knowing that Fournier was at that moment silently following me, I opened a door which did seem to be the most logical means of exit—but it was instead the entrance of a comfortable little bedroom.

"I beg your pardon, madam," I murmured.

The occupant of the room did not answer me. She lay there upon the large mahogany bed which loomed in the center of the chamber, and from the waist down her body was hidden from me by a rumpled sheet. Her head was turned away and an upflung arm hid her features from me. That portion of her body which was visible to me might as well have been naked, so skimpy was its covering, and I smiled at the sight of two rounded breasts beneath a sheer pajama vest.

And then I saw three round red marks upon the smooth flesh of one shoulder and my smile became a puzzled frown; behind me Paul Fournier said softly: "That is not the way to the street, my friend. That is — er — my wife's bedroom!"

Naturally at that moment I would have given a great deal to see the lady's face, for I was thinking as follows: "There can hardly be two women in Singapore at this time with fingerprints upon the identical same parts of their anatomies. This creature *must* be the Mrs. Smythe with whom I spent many pleasant moments not long ago!" But my curiousity was not satisfied. Startled by the sound of Fournier's voice, the woman hastily turned her back to us and pulled the sheet up with one hand. And then Fournier, with one hand hard upon my arm, was steering me to the door. And still I had not seen the lady's face.

THE next day I spoke as follows to my eminent Chinese friend, Lin Tsi: "Lin Tsi," I said, "I shall need a motor launch and a crew of three or four men. You will make the arrangements for me?"

"For you who have so often befriended me," said Lin Tsi, "I would arrange even to have my honorable ancestors disturbed in their graves."

And about midnight, Mrs. Smythe came again to visit me.

"Is it possible," I said, scowling, "that you are really the wife of Paul Fournier?"

She was apparently much surprised by my question. The color in her cheeks faded and she stood for a moment with one hand pressed hard against the udulating swell of her left breast. "You— recognized me last night?" she whispered.

"Then you *are* Mrs. Fournier?"

"I— yes, I am. But that makes no difference! I must get to Selatpandjang without Paul's knowledge!" And when I was slow to answer, she said softly: "Are you afraid of Paul?"

"Madam," I declared, "there are many things I am afraid of, but Paul Fournier is most assuredly not one of them. Now listen to me carefully. About one-half mile from the old Webley warehouse on the waterfront, there is an abandoned wharf which at one time was the property of the Yat Sun Trading Company. You are familiar with the place?"

"I know where it is, yes."

"Be there," I said, "at one a. m."

She did not seem in any great hurry to leave my apartment. Coming closer to me, she curled her arms gently about my neck and squirmed herself deliciously against me, in a manner that brought little beads of perpiration to my face and sent tingling sensations darting through my body.

I am at all time human, as I have remarked before, and when this exotic creature who was Paul Fournier's wife put her trembling red lips close to mine and whispered warmly, "Kiss me! Kiss me the way you did last night!" . . . I found immense delight in complying with her request.

"I am curious." I said presently, "about those marks on your shoulder. They are still there?"

"Look," she murmured, "for yourself."

Well, is was a simple matter indeed, for me to displace certain soft articles of her apparel and convince myself that the marks were still there upon the alabaster smoothness of her flesh.

And then, though the hour of midnight was drawing near, I yielded to the yearnings within me and put an arm about the woman's waist, drawing her closer to me. The warmth of her quivering body intoxicated me, and the soft sounds of delight that emanated from her lips were music indeed to my drugged senses . . .

MY eminent Chinese friend, Lin Tsi, had not let me down, and so, with an excellent motor launch and four trusted Malays to handle it, I arrived at the old Webly warehouse about twenty minutes after midnight. Rain had by that time begun to drizzle from the exceedingly black sky overhead, and the sea was in an ill mood. The trip across the Strait of Malacca to Selatpandjang would be no pleasure excursion.

I found Paul Fournier awaiting and cursing the lateness of my arrival. He had his own men there—unclean half-castes, most of them—to assist in loading the loot on board my admirable little vessel, and in ten minutes from the time of my arrival I was ready to cast off again.

"Remember now!" Fournier said to me, speaking with his face close to mine and forcing the words unpleasantly through his teeth. "This stuff is to be delivered in Selatpandjang, and I want a signed receipt from Agnew!"

"Indeed you shall have one," I murmured. "Indeed you shall."

"See that I get it!'

I was glad to be away from there, for it was obvious to me that Fournier had become a very nervous individual. To be sure, he had reason for being nervous. The bales of loot which now lay scattered around and about the deck of my little launch, each nicely wrapped in its waterproof covering, represented approximately ten times the amount of money he was paying me for transporting them.

Then again, the increasing rain and unsavory darkness were sufficient to make any man nervous, especially a man of Fournier's temperament. It is men like Fournier who get in trouble with the authorities. They lack poise.

I remember now that he shouted to me several times, repeatedly warning me to be careful of his precious cargo, while the launch was pulling away from the Webley warehouse. Then the darkness and the rain were kind enough to remove him from my sight, and I was in a private world of my own, with bales of excellent silks, as I have said, lying around and about me, and a crew of four trusted Malays awaiting my commands.

It was the work of but a moment to examine the bales to make certain that they were really waterproof. Having done that, I called the Malays to me and gave orders quietly, explaining my reasons for such orders, lest the men think me slightly insane.

The Malays—admirable fellows!—grinned when I had finished my explanations. Then, without protest, they went speedily to work, while the launch moved slowly through the night toward the abandoned wharf of the Yet Sun Trading Company.

"There will be weeping and wailing in

I knew one man who disappeared suddenly.

Singapore before this night is over," I thought. And I wondered if the wife of Paul Fournier would in truth be waiting upon the Yat Sun wharf.

IN twenty minutes the Malays came to me, drenched but still grinning, and announced that their work was finished. "Good!" I said. "You shall all be rewarded." Whereupon, leaving one of them at the wheel, I went into the cabin to procure whiskey—for there. is no reward in heaven or on earth more satisfying to our Malay brethren than a plentitude of whiskey with which to warm the belly.

In excellent spirits and humming to myself, I entered the cabin. And there, bless my soul, I stood staring in utter amazement. For my astonishing little friend of last evening, the young lady who called herself Regine, was standing there with practically no clothes on, smiling at me!

"I swam aboard," she said, "while your men and Fournier's were loading the launch at the warehouse. I'm going with you."

Now this was a predicament indeed, for I had already made arrangements to transport one female to Selatpandjang, and the cabin of my admirable little launch was hardly large enough to accomodate two of them. Yet, being at all times a gentleman, I was more concerned at this moment with the fact that my uninvited guest was obviously cold and uncomfortable.

Her clothes, dripping a great deal of the China Sea, were draped over the back of a chair, and the girl herself was shivering in an alarming manner. In fact she had shivered so much and so violently that both her enticing little breasts had almost worked free of the flimsy little band of gauze which was designed to enclose them.

Now Singapore is not the nicest place in the world in which to be overtaken with pneumonia, and as I have said before, I am at all times a gentleman. My duty as a gentleman was at this moment very clear to me. The lady was cold. She must be warmed. And since there was no stove in the cabin, I must attend to the warming personnally.

Removing her wet clothes from the chair, I seated myself there and drew Regine gently into my lap. "When this trembling little body of yours is warmer," I murmured, "you shall have dry clothes to wrap around it. It is a very lovely body, my dear."

She smiled, and said softly: "You are very kind to me." And she did not protest when I stroked her arms in an effort to restore their natural heat.

"Your lips are cold, also," I declared, touching them with my own. But they were soon very warm indeed. In fact their moist hungry pressure upon my mouth kindled enormous fires within my own body, and the longer I kissed this interesting little girl, the more intoxicated I became with the nearness of her.

There is no telling how far I might have gone if a warning hail from the deck hadn't informed me that there would be no time for further progress. However, the chill in Regine's snuggling body had long since evaporated before a surge of amazing warmth, and so, rising to my feet, I wrapped my own coat about her shoulders and said: "Why did you come here?"

"To be with you," she answered simply. "To be with you always. And to warn you."

"Warn me? Of what?"

"Fournier is up to something. What it is, I don't know, but Edmund Welch of the Singapore police is mixed up in it. You must be careful!"

"The Eel is always careful," I said. "And now you must hide. We are approaching a destination. You must hide here. There may be trouble." And unlocking a small compartment on the far side of the cabin, I bundled her into it, closing the door after her.

"She is a most charming young lady," I thought. "It will indeed be a pleasure to have her with me, especially if I am forced to leave Singapore in haste."

WHEN I went on deck, the launch had slackened speed and was droning gently toward the wharf of the Yat Sun Trading Company. In the darkness, the huge wharf piles were like black towers looming before us, and the sea was a heaving carpet, treacherous indeed. Without accident, however, the launch came to a stop on the sheltered side of the wharf and was lashed there by the four competent Malays who leaped to obey my orders.

"I doubt very much," I said aloud, "that Mrs. Paul Fournier will be among those waiting for me." And I was right.

The man I saw first was Fournier himself, and he came striding out of rain and darkness with Mr. Edmund Welch, of the local constabulary, at heel. Behind these two came others, who were all policemen. In the hands of Mr. Welch was a very formidable-looking machine gun.

"This is indeed a surprise," I said.

Paul Fournier had a nasty grin upon his unlovely face, and he said: "Sure it's a surprise, Eel. A bigger one than you anticipated, eh?" Mr. Edmund Welch, crowding behind him, scowled at me and said gutturally: "Step aside, Eel. This time you're trapped."

"May I ask what this is all about?" I said.

"You're under arrest for transporting stolen silks!" Welch snarled. Then he twisted his fat face into a most unpleasant leer and added: "It's a frame-up Eel, but it was the one sure way of nabbing you. We had this all figured out even before Fournier sent for you. He and I and the girl who works for him planned this whole coup very carefully—and you blundered right into it!"

"The girl who works for him," I murmured. "Ah, yes. You mean Fournier's wife."

They did not answer me. While Welch and Fournier forced me to stand there upon the wharf, with the muzzle of the machine gun watching over me, the policemen went on board my admirable little launch. They were very pompous policemen. They arrest my four Malays. Then they looked around in search of the bales of stolen silks.

TEN minutes later, when they had searched every inch of the deck and looked down into the cabin, the policemen were not so pompous. In fact, they were deeply bewildered and confused. One of them strode across the wharf and said to Welch: "Something has gone wrong, sir. The cargo is positively not on board!"

I was watching Mr. Welch's fat face at that moment, and even in the darkness I saw the face change color. It changed color with amazing rapidity, turning from its normal muddy gray to a deep scarlet, then to a pasty white. For a moment the man was quite unable to speak. Then thrusting himself closer to me, he sputtered: "You've tricked us!"

"But how?" I murmured. "Really, Mr. Welch, I came here merely to pick up a passenger. Fournier's wife, she said she was."

"She's not my wife!" Fournier raged.

Then I spoke as follows: "It is obvious," I said, "that you gentlemen have been to a great deal of trouble for nothing. First I was hired by Mr. Fournier to transport a cargo of silks to Selatpandjang. Then, as prearranged by you, I was approached by a lady who wished me to take *her* to Seatpandjang. It was a clever arrangement, gentlemen. Very clever indeed. But the silks seem to have vanished. That is a pity."

Now Mr. Edmund Welch is a man of intelligence, and realized that the fortunes of war indeed turned against him. Nevertheless, hs spent fifteen minutes parading wrathfully up and down the deck of the launch, seeking silks which were obviously not there. Finally, calling off his men who were guarding my four innocent Malays, he addressed himself to me as follows:

"You have won again, Eel," he said bitterly. "But remember—one of these days you will go too far. Now get out of here and take your miserable little launch with you!"

"It is an admirable little launch," I protested. And to Paul Fournier I said: "Please give my kindest regards to your wife."

(Continued on page 123)

Before he could dodge, the sword swished down. He could see it glitter in the moonlight, even as it cracked on his skull with blinding force.

The revenge of the French conqueror, the allure of the young Spanish traitress, live weirdly in the old dungeon and decide the fate of modern lovers

DRUMS of

THE year was 1680. Across the waters of Matanzas Bay filtered bright moonlight, the moonlight of Spanish Florida. Within the shadows of a palmetto grove the cavalier Jules Lavier talked to the Seminole chief, Nichosatti.

"It is madness," murmured the Indian. "They will kill thee, Lavier!"

Jules Lavier laughed softly. In the

By CHARLES R. ALLEN

DOOM ••

moon-bathed, tropical darkness his laugh had a musical ring, yet in no way did it blend with the tiger-like gleam in his eyes.

His brown hand closed over a shin-ing sword hilt and he stared toward the black hulk of Fort San Marco. A grim smile flitted across his handsome, adventurer's face. "Fear not, Nichosatti, The Spanish dogs must catch me ere they kill me!"

The Indian chief gazed somberly across a desolate stretch of cypress and palmettos toward the brooding, rambling pile that was San Marco.

"What is your plan?" he asked quietly.

"Just this," returned Jules Lavier. "For six days we have lain in this jungle edge, dying of fever. We might be here for six more, Nichosatti, and never come closer to San Marco than this. All the arrows and spears that ever came out of Macarasi cannot prevail against those stone walls. And while we die here, the Spanish dogs walk in comfort in the courtyard of San Marco!"

He paused, a steely glitter of hate leaping in his dark eyes. "Thou wilt stay here with the men, Nichosatti. I am going across to San Marco and crawl around the moat. I will find their weakest spot, and when I have found it I will return. Then Nichosatti, we shall take our spears and arrows and move forward together and attack. We shall triumph! Not a Spaniard but shall die when we pour into San Marco!"

Without further words Jules Lavier gripped the hard hand of the Seminole and glided off in the shadows. The great sad eyes of Nichosatti watched him go; saw the moonlight glimmer faintly on his shining coat of armor. Then with a slight rustling noise he was gone; was swallowed up in the night.

A GREAT heaviness settled on the heart of the chieftain. None but he realized what a savior to the enslaved Indians was this Jules Lavier—this grim, smiling, swashbuckling, dangerous cavalier who had led them in many a bloody conquest against the Spaniards.

Out of a clear sky this lean French warrior had come to take up their hopeless cause against the brutal yoke of Spain.

Two years before Jules Lavier had landed in Spanish St. Augustine with a crew of pirates. A bewitching senorita had enthralled him. He had married her, had a son. In a fierce land of jungle, warfare, and fever he had set up a home.

Then came the great massacre of Macarasi. The bloodthirsting Spanish dons had wiped out a huge Indian settlement; butchered hundreds of their warriors, squaws, and children; had enslaved hundreds more and put them to the whip.

Jules Lavier they had accused as a traitor. They had murdered his wife, destroyed his home. But his little son, Juan Lavier, had been overlooked and rescued by a Seminole tribe, and carried to safety in the jungles.

Then came Jules Lavier to the Indians with only a seething revenge in his heart and took up the cause of the enslaved and tortured against the iron hand of the Spanish.

CRAWLING on hands and knees across a cypress swamp, Lavier left the jungles behind. He glided noiselessly through a stretch of tall grass and came out before the battlements of Ft. San Marco. To cross that open space in the bright moonlight would be to invite certain death from the Spanish muskets.

Even now he was so close to the fort he saw moonlight reflected on the ugly cannon muzzles and heard the clanking of swords and armor as Spanish soldiers walked the battlements and crossed the courtyard.

Withdrawing his steel rapier he moved along the edge of the tall grass patch, keeping well in the shadows. It would be better, he decided, to creep down the hill that ended at Mantanzas Bay. There, he could wade through the shallow water and come up on San Marco from the Bay side.

Like a flitting ghost he moved, under the very shadow of the grim fort. Half sliding, half walking, he stumbled down a steep grassy bank. He paused, listened. Only the faint lap-lap of water came to his ears.

Gliding forward again he crept almost to the water's edge, then halted abruptly with a hissing intake of breath. On the ground before him a shadowy human shape moved, rose up from the grass.

Jules Lavier swung back his steel sword, prepared to lunge forward. Yet before he could strike a soft voice spoke from the shadows—a low-pitched, tremulous girl's voice! "Who art thou?"

Lavier lowered his sword, moved closer. His brown, battle-bright eyes widened. It was a girl! A girl alone on that shadow-bathed hill; a soft lovely senorita, with glowing eyes and with raven tresses that tumbled down over her shoulders to lie on her tight-fitting velvet bodice.

Full, rounded breasts made a prominent bulge in that bodice, created a mound of feminine softness from which Lavier could not for the moment tear his eyes.

The Spanish girl took a step toward him—a movement revealed a sensuous litheness of hips and legs. Almost before Lavier she paused, her smouldering brown eyes surveying him; her ripe, passion-curved lips slightly parted in wonderment.

TO THE fighting savior of the Indians anything Spanish was an anathema, but there was an alluring spell of femininity about this girl that softened hate.

"I almost killed thee," he whispered.

"Who art thou? And what dost thou here?"

"I am Dolores," she said simply. "Daughter of Don Cervano. I like to sit here and watch the moonlight on the water. Thou art one of my father's men?"

"No," snapped Lavier. Mechanically his eyes wandered back to that swelling bodice; to the curved feminine mounds that pushed outward. There was something entrancing about those lovely hills; something that cooled Jules Lavier's fighting instincts, replaced it with growing desire. The girl herself was a lovely vision of simplicity and wide-eyed innocence that at once aroused in Lavier a torment of memory.

"Know you not?" he said harshly, "It is dangerous for thee to be here alone? There are many enemies of thy father's, creeping through these jungles at night!"

Dolores Cervano smiled. "I am not afraid. They would not harm me."

"No? Think thou not?" A cold reckless smile hovered on the lips of the cavalier, Lavier. It was a smile that many ladies along the Spanish main had seen, and cringed before, and yet in their hearts had admired.

Advancing, Lavier seized her wrist, slid a steel-sheathed arm about her slim waist. Slowly he drew her body close to his. Tighter and tighter he pressed it, until the swelling curves of her breasts were crushed against his iron-clad chest. Her trembling, ripe red lips hovered dangerously close to his; the warm softness of her round legs seemed to melt against him. "For a Spaniard," he murmured, "thou are indeed beautiful."

Dolores struggled to release herself from that grip of steel, found it impossible. Finally she lay impassive in his arms and continued to gaze at him with warm brown eyes.

"And if I were to kiss thee, Dolores —thou would not be afraid?"

Receiving no answer, Lavier tilted her pretty head back, sought the quivering softness of her lips. The contact was electric. Idly he had sought them but madly he clung to them, draining their hot nectar.

Tighter and tighter he felt the straining embrace of the Spanish girl. Her white arms slipped around his neck, drew his head down.

IN THAT strange moment the world stood still for Lavier. He was conscious only of a sweet curving feminine body pressed close to his. He ran exploring fingers along a smooth velvet-clad back, permitted his arm to encompass all her waist. Trembling, he drew her ever closer until their bodies were almost as one.

Wedged against his mouth her lips writhed suddenly in an excess of emotion and her legs shifted with a torturous motion. Lavier pressed curving flesh with convulsive fingers, kissed the upturned lips until blood pounded madly through his veins.

Dolores Cervano gave a low moan of ecstasy and shuddered. Her shudder, like a wave, communicated itself to his body. And Lavier found the satin-softness of her a thing of exquisite wonder. Gripping her arching body around the middle, he pressed her painfully close, while the flame of her lips sent his mind reeling.

"Wait—wait," she breathed. "We might be discovered here."

Impetuous, fiery, Lavier nodded. Along the adventurer's path he had found much that enthralled him, but this strange girl that had appeared like a wraith out of the moonlight fired his blood as nothing else had.

It was not in Lavier's make-up to question what might to another seem strange and unnatural. His was a spirit that took life as he found it. And so, with but one thought in his mind he permitted Dolores Cervano to lead him by the hand along the water's edge and finally up a steep slope.

"There is a grove of trees above," she murmured in the darkness. "Within them there will be no moonlight. There —." Pausing, her eloquent hand pressure made words seem futile.

Nearing the protecting shadow of a huge oleander bush Dolores Cervano released Lavier's hand. Only then did the adventurer realize he was in danger, but it was too late. Abruptly the girl darted away from him, screaming: "Rafael! Ricardo!"

LAVIER saw two burly Spanish guards leap from the shadows of the bush. Moonlight glittered on their heavy, long swords. He whipped out his own sword, stood his ground, cursing bitterly. It was not that he was trapped, and should die, but that he had been led into the trap by a woman's guile.

With a clash of steel the two Spaniards were upon him. Lavier poised, lunged forward, snaking his sword in and out with lightning-like movements. The clash of steel on steel grew louder. The Spaniards soon found they were matched against a deadly swordsman, a man whose nerves were iron; who fought with a calm, dangerous precision.

Fighting desperately, bitterly, Lavier was forced back, inch by inch. A blade cut the air with terrific force, sliced his arm, sent blood spurting. Another drove straight for his head. He parried the blow smashed the blade aside and ducked.

Coming up from a crouching position he shot forward like a spring released. Before the nearest of the two guards could recover from his last lunge, Lavier's sword sank deep in his chest. Convulsively, the Spaniard gripped at the

"Dolores! Judas!" he cried, and his fingers were like steel at her soft throat.

protruding blade, while blood spewed from his mouth. He staggered back, sank to the ground, but the other, seeing Lavier now standing weaponless snarled out a hoarse cry of triumph.

Swinging up his heavy sword for the final blow that would end the adventurer's life he leaped forward. Lavier crouched low, hurled his body at the stocky, oncoming legs. The two men crashed together with a dull thud; the sword whipped down, sliced Lavier's ankle. Lavier, with his arms wrapped around his opponent's middle, surged upward in a great heave. The feet of the bearded Spaniard left the ground suddenly. For a moment he clung like a great cat to Lavier's shoulders, then the latter hurled him down with smashing, stunning force.

Immediately, Dolores Cervano screamed out a summons for more men. Lavier heard them coming; heard the rattle of chains as a gate in Fort San Marco opened and a stream of men poured out.

He fought madly to disentangle himself from the fallen Spaniard, but the latter, aware of the approaching re-inforcements, only clung tighter to Lavier's wounded arm. At last the adventurer tore one fist free. He balled it, smashed it savagely against the Spaniard's chin. There was a dull crack of bone and the man sagged back—limp, senseless.

Scrambling to his feet, Lavier darted away. He had taken barely three strides when Dolores Cervano appeared beside him. The moonlight glittered on one of the broad swords which she held in both hands, high above her head. Before he could dodge or change his gait, the sword swished down, caught him full across the legs. Pain numbing his body Lavier sprawled on the grass and a moment later a dozen men pounced on him.

Something cracked on his skull with blinding force. In a fast-falling void of blackness he heard the boastful voice of Dolores Cervano: "I knew he was Jules Lavier as soon as I saw him! No longer will he plague my father's men. . . ."

IT WAS a steady beating of drums that finally brought Jules Lavier from a coma-like sleep. He opened his eyes, saw nothing but inky darkness. Fiery darts of pain shot through his limbs and his throat felt constricted, dry, swollen. He stretched out a hand, encountered a slimy stone wall.

Crawling about on all fours he discovered stone walls on all sides and realized with sinking heart he was in the ante room of death—in one of the prison dungeons of Fort San Marco. Vaguely, as from a distance he heard again the martial roll of drums. He knew what that meant too, and he braced his shoulders philosophically.

Don Cervano, pompous commander of San Marco had a sadistic flair for hanging prisoners. And as a prelude to this dramatic ceremony, it was his custom to have a rolling of drums and a flare of trumpets in the courtyard.

That the drums spelled doom for him, Lavier knew only too well. And that their booming was already in progress meant his hour had arrived. He clenched his fists until the nails tore his palms, stared unseeingly into the darkness.

Gradually, a great engulfing desire seared him. Revenge! To have that lovely female Judas at his side again—the girl who with her body had betrayed him into the hands of the Spaniards! To feel his finger sink into that soft, smooth throat! To pay her back in kind! Such was the fiery nature of the cavalier, Lavier. And such were his last thoughts.

It was not until the rolling of drums abruptly ceased that he realized how close death was. And being, in his own tempestuous and romantic way a religious man he made a last hasty concession to his faith.

IN a corner of the dungeon he found a small, sharp rock. With it he hacked at the wall until he had made what he conceived to be a cross. Then he knelt before it and offered up a short prayer for the guidance of his little son, Juan, left helpless in the hands of the Seminole Indians.

He was still praying when the guards arrived. Roughly they dragged him forth, tied his hands behind his back. He was led to the courtyard. In the cold, early light of dawn, phantomlike figures moved about and in a far corner loomed the gallows, gray and grim.

The drums rolled again as he was taken up the wooden steps. The hangman placed a noose over his neck, drew it tight, awaited the signal from Don Cervano.

Lavier glanced around the courtyard. He saw Don Cervano and beside him the slim form of his daughter Dolores. In the dark face of the girl was an expression of cruel satisfaction, the same expression that Judas himself must have worn in the garden.

Lavier smiled. A contemptuous, cavalier's smile that lighted up his whole handsome face in scorn. "Spanish swine!" he said.

Don Cervano gave a curt signal. The body of Jules Lavier dangled at the end of a rope. His dying lips worked convulsively. Could they have formed words they would have been: "Juan—Juan—my little son! What will become of thee!"

THE year was 1936. Under a summer sun the streets of St. Augustine lay hot and bright. John Lavery paused at the corner of Bay Street and San Marco Avenue, then stepped off the curb in the path of an oncoming Packard. The dark-haired, sloe-eyed girl seized his arm, jerked him back: "For heaven's sake, John! Do you want to get killed? What's wrong with you?"

John Lavery stepped to the curb again, stared down into the pretty face of his wife. His eyes were lost in distance, far away. "Nothing—nothing's wrong, Doris. I was just—thinking."

"About what?"

"This town—St. Augustine. There's something strange about it. I can't put it in words—I just feel it."

"Why, I think it's a nice place for a honeymoon," she pouted.

"Oh sure." John Lavery managed a faint smile. "I didn't mean that. I meant this old town seems to be full of ghosts!"

"Ghosts?" Her tone was startled.

"Yes. I don't know how to explain, but seeing all these funny crooked streets and the old houses—centuries old, most of them. . . ." Pausing, his voice trailed off and a slight frown settled on his handsome face. He pointed to an ancient slave market across the street and then to the distant tower of Fort Marion, jutting out proudly over Matanzas Bay

"It seems to me," he continued, "Ghosts are walking through those places. The ghosts of old Spanish dons and senoritas, rigged out in all their ruffles and silks and armor. It seems to me these streets are full of them—that they are standing around, watching us."

His pretty wife of three days standing backed away from him, alarm beginning to trouble her Spanish eyes. "John, are you ill? You never talked like this before!"

John Lavery sighed, glanced at her queerly. "This is an old, old town, Doris. Think of the centuries of bloodshed, of wars, of massacres these streets have seen."

She tossed her dark head impatiently. Sidling up to him she tucked his arm through hers, pressed it inward until the back of his hand felt the warmth of her yielding breast. Her eyes sparkled roguishly "Stop it, John! You're getting actually clairvoyant. Pay some attention to me!"

(Continued on page 106)

Thieves'

By Lorenz Mendez

The old bandit had ravished the gold of Mexico for his private hoard, and now feminine wiles sought his secret. Then men came down from the mountain, and mystery worked by night . . . settling the fate of two faithless women

ONCE a month Juan Garcia, the voiceless one, threw his colored *zarape* about his shoulders, mounted his grey mule and rode down the mountainside to Balsas to drink his fill of *tequila* in the *cantina* of Mamasita Diega. For two days he would squat in the shadows of the tumbledown little saloon and drink the fiery juice of the cactus—and always he paid for it with good silver pesos. One spent, he reached

Justice

His package burst open and the
two heads met their eyes.

into the bosom of his old cotton shirt and
clinked out another, round, hard, and
gleaming.

Mamasita Diega wasn't the only one
who marveled at the endless source of
Juan's peso supply. The whole town
wondered, for it was well known Juan
stooped to no labor. Back up the mountain at the Mina de los Angeles, where
Juan lived with his young wife, they
watched him like a hawk. But saying
nothing and hearing nothing, he sat in
the shade of his 'dobe hut all day long
and gazed serenely at the tropical mountainside, while his wife, Cuca, who was
the daughter of Mamasita Diega herself,

searched fruitlessly for the old man's
treasure.

His fellow countrymen, who worked
in the mine, liked him. He tended to
his own business, he was free with his
money, and though he neither spoke nor
heard they liked to have him around.
"*Sordo mudo,* deaf mute," they would
say to any wondering stranger and shrug
nonchalantly when Juan paid silver pesos
for their pleasure.

TONIGHT Juan lay on his back
beside the still figure of his young
wife and stared into the darkness. For
three hours he had laid thus waiting

patiently for Cuca to go to sleep. A mountain breeze whipped through the pines and cedars, stirred a night bird into flight.

Juan raised softly on his elbow to peer at the woman beside him. Softly he laid brown fingers on the lemon-colored mounds of her breasts, not in caress, but to note the evenness of her breathing. Apparently satisfied he arose, stepped noiselessly into his clothes. At the doorway he turned for a last look at the sleeper.

Pear-shaped breasts rose and fell regularly, but hardly was Juan out the door before she, too, rolled swiftly to her slim feet. From the darkened window she watched him trudge toward the corner of the yard, disappear into the shadows cast by a mango tree.

Like a shadow she crept from the back door, fled swiftly down the wavering path that led to the quarters of the mine workers. A whistle, low but shrill, emitted from between her white teeth. Again.

A blacker shadow joined her, slipping silently from a shack. Quickly the two shadows merged into one as the newcomer took Juan's faithless wife into his arms. For a moment he held her close, but her mouth pulled away from his passionate kiss to whisper excitedly in his ear.

"He is fixing to go off tomorrow, the old one! Now he is after his money again. You must follow him, Joselito, to see where he has it stored. Quickly!"

Together they ran back toward the little hut, crept soundlessly around the corner.

Juan squatted half in the moonlight, half in the shadows of the thick tree. Silver gleamed in his hand, tinkled like a bell, as he counted the pesos that had been stored in the hollow hole. Then in wordless pantomime he shook his head, arose, thrust a hand deep in the hollow bowl of the mango tree.

It emerged with a rag-covered machete which gleamed bright and wickedly in the moonlight. The skinny old man withdrew it from the dirty wrapper, thrust it carelessly through his wide leather belt. He trudged away toward the side of the looming mountain.

"Now," gloated Cuca to her lover. "Now!" But he, cautious, held her back until Juan disappeared completely. Then together they ran toward the hollow tree.

Jose's searching fingers found nothing but the rags which had covered the machete. Disappointed they stood silently for a moment. Suddenly Cuca's arms were about him, her eyes gleamed again.

"Up the mountain after him, *chulo!* The old goat must have it up there, must only bring a little to his cache each time."

Another kiss, a few more caresses, and the man trotted down the trail after Juan, the speechless one. He went silently, cautiously, once pausing to loosen the gleaming knife at his belt. There were stories about this Juan Garcia and it paid a young man in love to be careful! It was often rumored that this same Garcia had ridden at the right hand of the famous *bandido*, Zapata, not so many years ago, when the scourge of Mexico was at the height of his power!

But now Juan seemed merely an old man, deaf and dumb, who walked carelessly up a mountain path with no of followers. Jose sneered to himself, remembered the man's affliction and walked less cautiously behind him.

A SWINGING bridge spanned the roaring mountain stream that furnished power for the mine. Straight across this bridge went Juan, made a sudden turn to the right. As soon as he disappeared into the underbrush Jose trotted across the bridge after him wondering where the old fool was taking him, where he had his silver hid. Once he, Jose, had that silver, he could take Cuca away. Perhaps it might be better to kill the old fool? Wronged husbands, you know, and all that.

Around the edge of a cliff path, and suddenly the heavens fell on Jose, the betrayer. He pitched forward on his face, groaned once and lay still. Above him, eyes narrowed, gleaming like those of a beast, leaned Juan Garcia, the man of no speech, *who knew he had been followed.*

Strange, rumbling sounds came from his throat, he shook his fist at the fallen man. For a moment he seemed to listen, to peer about, to await farther pursuit, and evidently became satisfied that Jose was his only follower. Again the younger man moaned and stirred on the rocky ground.

Suddenly a flash in the moonlight, the sickening crunch of steel against bone, steel sheering through flesh and tendon. The body of Jose, the betrayer, quivered, crimson welled from his neck in great splurges. The head rolled away down the slight slope until Juan stopped it with his foot, kicked it carelessly into a clump of bushes.

For a long while the killer stood there staring down at the corpse, his eyes gleaming, his nostrils quivering. Presently he drew off his own *zarape* to staunch the blood at the severed neck. With unbelievable strength for a skinny old man he dragged the body through the shrubbery to the edge of the river. The *zarape* well looped about it, he filled the gaping folds with rocks, shoved the corpse over the bank. It splashed in the white-capped torrent, seemed to bounce momentarily then disappear.

Juan spat disdainfully into the water, turned back to the scene of battle.

For moments he worked skillfully kicking loose shale and rock across the bloodstained path, trodding them carefully into place. Then he snatched up the severed head by the matted hair, threw back his own bony head to laugh soundlessly. The white eyes of his wife's lover glared back at him. He picked up the hat, took another cautious look about and disappeared up the dim trail, the gruesome head in his hand.

DAWN was just breaking over the mountains when Cuca sighed in her feigned sleep and moved aside to let her husband lay down beside her. He did not touch her, did not so much as glance at her. But with full daylight she satisfied her burning curiosity, found what had clattered so loudly on the dresser when he returned.

There were three neat piles of silver pesos. Behind them lay a machete, the long square blade covered with black stickins. Beside the machete—a human ear black with dried blood. She touched the ear fearfully, shuddered and glanced toward her husband. He lay flat on his back, black eyes staring at her.

Even when she found later in the day that Jose, her lover, did not return to his work in the mines she was afraid to say anything to the grim-eyed, silent man who was her husband.

About noon Juan saddled his grey mule, rode down the mountain to the town. Mamasita Diega greeted him with open arms and reached for her best *tequila*. She asked about her daughter on a dirty piece of paper with a stub of a pencil, and Juan shrugged disdainfully and went on with his *tequila*. Acquaintances greeted him, were treated to drinks, remaining to slap his shoulder and invite their friends to partake.

"*Sordo mudo*," they explained jovially, "a deaf mute, but a prince of a fellow!" '

TWO days later Juan rode home trembling and shaking to retire to the hammock in the front yard and sleep deeply with his mouth wide open. Cautiously Cuca probed his pockets, found not so much as a silver peso.

Jim Curtis, American manager of the Minas de los Angeles, cursed his own wife that same morning. His eyes were as red-rimmed as Juan's his fingers as shaking and nervous.

"Money! Money! Money," he swore, slapping the breakfast table until the chocolate cups jumped and rattled. "Damn it, that's all I hear, money. What do you do with it? Where, in this God-forsaken place, could you spend it? Lorraine, I'm telling you frankly I'm in the red. There'll be no seashore, no Acapulco or Matzatlan this year. We'll have to take it easy."

She sat white-faced across the table from him, the sheer negligee loose about her breasts, as they rose and fell angrily. Her lips were taunting, her eyes angry.

"I suppose you're short in your accounts again? Must have spent more than you meant to on the señoritas in Mexico City last month! If you'd tend to your own business instead of theirs maybe your wife could afford the things—".

He leaped to his feet, shoved the table angrily. She caught herself, managed to keep from falling with an effort. Then he was on her, her white shoulders turning red beneath his fingers as he shook her. The solitary clasp of her negligee gave way, her breasts sprang forth to quiver and tremble. He released her suddenly and she slapped his face, hard, then drew back aghast at the look of rage that overspread his features.

"You! You!" he managed to sputter, feeling his throbbing cheek. "I ought to kill you. Telling me about my señoritas. Why you're a joke, a laugh! I bring you up here into a savage country and even then you can't forget your habits. You parade half-naked before the peons, you try your charms and your wiles on the lowest of them all! And then you accuse me of having women. Someday I'm going to have the game as well as the name!"

She sneered, walked away, her hips liquid with indignation. Down the hallway a doorway slammed. Curtis stood quivering in his rage, his knuckles white on the table edge. On noiseless feet Cuca entered, a carafe and glass in her brown hands. She had been listening at the door. Her red lips were provocative, her white teeth flashed as she smiled at him.

"Your *equila*, señor." Her voice was soft, a challenge. He seized the liquor, tossed it off and poured another glass, dismissing her with a wave of her hand. She leaned low over the table knowing that his eyes would seek the deep valley between her pear-shaped breasts, that her low cut waist disclosed the upper slopes of lemon-colored mounds. She did not look at him but felt his eyes on her swaying hips as she left the room.

CUCA was convinced that one man alone, James Curtis himself, could help her against that sorry brute of a husband who had too many pesos for his own good. She went about her work with that end in view, being certain that at all times Jim Curtis had every opportunity to observe her lithe charms.

Curtis, bitter at his wife, viewed those generous charms with evident approval.

After all, just as he had told Lorraine, why not have the game as well as the name? Curtis' main weakness was capped and corked in bottles. The recent trip to Mexico City had played hob with a great amount of money, true enough, but the señoritas had profited but little. Most of it had gone across green-topped tables and mahogany bars. But—if his wife meant to accuse him of cheating—well—!

He soon acquired the habit of making excuses to touch Cuca. On the second day he was bold enough to brush a lush hip as if by accident, and thrilled when

While he waited, she lowered herself into the icy water.

she did not move away. She smiled, smouldering fires in her eyes, a promise on her pouting mouth.

Farther up on the mountain side old Juan sat serenely in the shade waiting for the end of the month. He watched the time spent by his young wife at her toilet, noted the pains she took in arraying herself, the care she spent in reddening her already carmine lips, powdering her smooth cheeks. He used to grin at her evilly and sometimes, when she overdid the thing, he would draw a twisted, whorled piece of dried flesh from his shirt and fondle it in her presence. Inevitably she shuddered and ran out of the house. In her heart she wondered how he, a deaf mute, had ever learned that Jose was her lover.

Three days later Jim Curtis dropped his pen. He leaned for it at the same time that Cuca stooped to the floor. Their heads met in a resounding crash and Cuca sat down abruptly. They laughed together for a moment before Jim leaned and kissed her forehead.

That was the beginning, for in the next second she was in his arms, her hot mouth parting to receive his tremulous kiss, her hands pulling him closer and closer to her moving mouth. Her pear-shaped breasts flattened, burned against his chest, and her hips shivered beneath the thin blackness of her scanty skirt.

ANOTHER week and she was slipping away to meet him in the flowered *patio*, when Lorraine Curtis, the wife, and Juan Garcia, the husband, were fast asleep. She learned his money troubles, he learned her marital woes, and they consoled each other during long moonlit nights when the cool mountain breezes were more than necessary to cool the heat of their blood.

"Money, money," groaned Curtis one night, her body pressed hotly against his. "If I just had the money I could take you away from here!"

She kissed him hotly, whispered something in his ear, but he laughed.

"A few pesos wouldn't take us far, Cuca. We'll have to have more than Juan's little savings!"

Her eyes grew dreamy; she sat up straighter. "It isn't just a few pesos," she said. "Long years ago Juan was a *bandido*, rode with Zapata and his cutthroat brother. Three times they took Mexico City. This I know for truth. Juan has money put away; more than you may think!"

Curtis' eyes were also greedy now. The girl continued.

"The peons say Zapata himself hid his treasure in the caves here in Guerrero, all in silver, pesos, and plate."

"What happened to Zapata?"

"He was killed before he could come back for his treasure. My mother, who knows everyone for many years, says Juan rode with Zapata as his aide. What if Juan knew the big cache, the real hiding place? From somewhere he gets silver pesos every month! It would be easy to follow him!"

Curtis still remained silent. Cunningly Cuca said, "And then we could go away together, just you and I!"

As her lips found his, as he pressed her tumultuous body to him, a dark figure moved away from the doorway leading into the *patio*.

THREE minutes later Lorraine Curtis lit a cigarette in the darkness of her room and smiled to herself. At last she had caught her husband in a compromising situation! And further than that— sometimes there was something to these tales of peons told! She, too, knew Juan had plenty of pesos at all times but had never given the fact much thought. What if the old Mexican did know Zapata's cache, the place the famous rider used as a storehouse for the three million silver pesos accumulated over his years as a *bandido?*

Perhaps Juan wondered a little bit at the sudden rise of his fortunes, or perhaps he was content to take the breaks and ask no questions. When Señor Curtis insisted on his coming into the big house to drink with him, Juan accepted gravely and over many thimble-like glasses of *tequila* the mine manager and the deaf mute wrote messages back and forth.

Curtis claimed to be interested in the history of the mountainous state. He wrote: "Juan, tell me something about Zapata, the bandit. Did he operate through this section?"

Juan replied painfully, pencil in his skinny, gnarled fingers.

"Señor, I have heard that but I do not know.'

Curtis looked at him and laughed, shrugging his shoulders good-naturedly. He poured another drink before writing:

"You joke, Juan. I have information that *you* rode with Zapata yourself, rode at his right hand!"

Juan's eyes were a little narrow, he grinned like a wolf, his red tongue clicking. "You joke, señor! I am a peon, no *bandido!*"

And so it stood.

A DAY or two later, attired in a pair of flaring riding breeches that tapered about rounded knees and lowered thighs, Lorraine was a visitor at Juan's house. Juan lay sleepy-eyed in the hammock beneath the trees. Lorraine called Cuca, told her Curtis wanted her at the house. Cuca departed with never a backward glance, glad of the opportunity to be with her lover.

A chair stood close to the hammock. Lazily Lorraine drew a cigarette from the pocket of her half open shirt, lit it, trickled blue smoke from her nostrils. She put one booted leg on the chair, leaned toward Juan. His black eyes swept over the half-revealed mounds of blue-veined white flesh, the deep, dusky valley between. Her eyes were a challenge to his, her lips were parted eagerly.

"I think you are a *bandido!*" she snapped suddenly, sharply.

A blank expression appeared on Juan's coffee-colored face. He sat up quickly, pointed to his open mouth, to his right ear, shook his head sorrowfully and shrugged. Lorraine laughed. This time she drew a pad and pencil from her pocket, wrote:

"Do you know the mountain-side well? Could you guide me to good fishing spots along the river?"

Juan raised black brows in surprise. For a year the *gringo* lady had been in this paradise of nature without showing any interest in her surroundings. Now, fishing! He nodded, however, and wrote clumsily:

"*Si, señora,* Juan can guide you. When?"

"After *siesta*, today," she wrote. "We walk the mountainside."

He nodded, smiled his wolfish smile and accepted a cigarette. She leaned very close to him to give him a light, looked long and meaningly in his black, beady eyes. When she left, she touched the back of his hand with her white fingers.

THE end of the month approached and Cuca and Curtis laid their plans. She did not tell Curtis that Jose had followed the old man last month and failed to return. She was afraid he would back out. But she promised to come directly to the house and tell him when Juan departed on his monthly journey.

Lorraine, too, knew that the end of the month would bring action. But she relied on her charm, on the lush ripeness of her mature body, the white softness of her tantalizing curves. Never had she

(Continued on page 109)

He is a prisoner on the road to Temiltepan—the road from which no one returns. But he goes willingly, knowing that Morenita has not forsaken him

By
JOHN
BARD

BLOOD
on the

MORENITA

then from the other *prisioneros*. All at once something sharp smacks me on the kisser and I sit up like a spring tension jack knife.

Being no moon it's black as pitch but I hear a rattle like a pebble rolling across the floor. I feel around until my hand comes in contact with something small and hard that crackles when I pick it up. I unwrap the piece of paper and toss the pebble into the corner. Lifting up the *petate* to shield the light from the door, I strike a *cerillo*. By its flare I read:

I AM trying to snooze between fleas on a *petate* laid against the stone floor of an army *carcel* this side of Temiltepan. I can hear a snore now and

DOORSTEP

95

"Potfull on ice for sticks bodyguard
Big shot lams jenny push it."

It is signed by number nineteen. He must have thrown it through the little window up near the ceiling. I cuss as I translate the slang code. I'm in a helluva position to help the governor get south in a plane with a pot full of jack to pay his soldiers. I'm lucky if I can help myself.

"Hissssssssst!" says a low voice.

I almost jump out of my shoes. I roll up the code message, take a deep breath, and swallow it. I am expecting somebody to rub me out during the night so I sort of pull in my belly muscles and get ready to take it, but I don't say anything.

"Hissssssssst . . . Americano!"

I grunt. "What do you want?"

"Com to the cell door, please, and be ver' quiet."

"Nuts, Mex. You can shoot me from there."

"But . . . I don' want to shoot the Americano." Long silence. "I want to . . . kiss him."

Ain't that a hot one? I get a mental picture of two long black mustachios drooping out of a solemn greasy phiz. Well, hell! It can't be a *woman* in a military jail at two o'clock in the morning! What am I going to think?

"All right," I say, "but get this. If you're a man, you get a nice juicy poke in the teeth."

I hear a low chuckle as I finally manage to reach the cell door through the dense blackness. It don't sound feminine to me.

"Listen," I say, "I can't see a thing. Just cancel this kiss business."

"You don' need to see to kiss."

"The hell I don't!"

"Give me your hands, Americano."

"What's the idea?"

"I go to prove to you that I am woman. Give me your hands."

I SHOVE my paws through the bars expecting any second to have somebody stick a knife between my ribs. My fingers come into sudden contact with something silky and warm that pulses rapidly like a frightened rabbit. Silk, with soft flesh underneath! *Por Dios,* it *is* a woman! My hands lift up, and now it's a woman's bare shoulders. I clasp my fingers spasmodically; my breath goes out with a hiss.

An ecstatic shiver passes through my fingers, up my arms, down my spine. I fall against the bars of the door and pull her to them. Between the interlacing of the bars I can feel the warmth of her round firm body, the sweetness of her feminine figure.

After a while I hear her low contralto whisper.

"Am I a woman?"

"Phewww; If I were as much a man!"

"Oh, Sangre Brown, you *are.*"

"Wha . . . say, how do you know my name?"

"Tsk, tsk. Morenita do not feel ver' flatter'. In the afternoon I om rescue and in the night I am forget."

"What! . . . Well, I'm a son of a gunman. I didn't recognize your voice. Are you the girl the *capitán*. . . ?"

"I am Morenita. The *capitán* desire me. The *capitán* will have me. He say so himself. But the Americano, he is *caballero.* He say, 'Nots to you, greeser!' "

"Nuts."

"*Sí,* nots. And the *capitán* say, 'Greengo, you go to die!' And now, the *capitán* he is in bed, the Greengo he is in *carcel,* and Morenita she is in the

Greengo's arms. . . Ohhh, they feel so strong."

"How did you get in here?" I whisper.

"I tell the guard I am your girl and give him hundred pesos. I offer him thousand pesos if you escape, but he say if you escape, he will be shoot because the *capitán* is ver' mad."

I crush her to me till I know the bars must bruise her firm, full breasts.

"Why'd you bother to see me?"

"Because I love you."

"Yeah . . . but, what else?"

She sobs just once. "Tomorrow you take the road to Temiltepan."

I don't say anything for a minute, but my muscles tense. I know what it means to take the road to Temiltepan.

I say, "So it's the *ley de fugo* for Blood Brown."

There isn't a sound but I can tell she's sobbing by the quivering of her warm velvety lips against mine.

"*Sí . . . la ley de fugo.*"

M̲Y UPPER lip comes up against my nose. "So the brown-bellied runts want to wipe me out with the 'law of flight.' They're going to give me a chance to run and then shoot me in the back. The hell they will! Old Hardhead gave me a job to do down here, and no *frijole* eatin' spig is goin' to rub me out until it's done. Listen, Morenita, can you get back in here again?"

"Until the guard is change."

"Here, take this two hundred pesos. The hundred you're out and another in case you have to grease the guard again. Come on now, no argument! Take it!"

"*Bien*, but what does Morenita do?"

"Bring me a pack of Monte Carlos . . . some dry Marijuana. . . ."

"Only Marijuano . . . ?"

"And some pulverized *chiles rojas*. . . ."

"I will pulverize them myself."

"Then, I want you to go to Temiltepan. You have to get there before daylight. Find number six Avenida Pulsonente. There is a brass knocker in the center of the door. Don't use that. Use the rusty knocker that is off to one side. Rap six times, then repeat it. A peon in a pink blouse will come to the door. Tell him. . . ."

I pause a minute to be sure I phrase it right. Morenita speaks eagerly as she pulls closer to me. "*Sí, sí* . . . what I shall tell him?"

"Tell him there will be blood on his doorstep when he amputates the leg."

I̲T is dawn. Though it is still dark in my cell I can tell by the shuffle of feet. The guard is changing. Someone stops outside the door. I hear a rattle of heavy keys and the squeak of rusty hinges.

"*Ven, Gringo!*"

I get up slowly from my *petate* and walk casually to the door. I can faintly make out three men, an officer and two privates. As I reach the doorway the officer bows with mock profundity and steps aside. His lips are lifted in a sneer as he speaks.

"*Pase Ud. Caballero.*"

Then I recognize the voice. I can't resist it. I say, "Glad you were able to get here this morning, *capitán*."

His teeth click together but he controls himself.

"I cannot bear to have my so distinguished guest depart without I wish him *feliz viaje*."

"I am sure I shall enjoy my journey."

He grins crookedly.

"I am so sorry I cannot conduct you

personally to your . . . ah . . . destination."

"No doubt, *capitán,* your excellent *compadres* will know the way."

"*Sí, caballero,* Bartolo and José know the way. It is a very simple one."

As I shift my eyes to the sour-pussed privates standing sloppily at attention I reflect that it would have to be a simple one. I can see they hold me personally responsible for getting them up before breakfast.

"You will forgive us if we search you?"

"Hell, yes," I say, as Bartolo, gentle as his ancestors, the Aztec Priests, gives me a thorough combing, "if you find anything valuable let me know."

Bartolo produces a *bronc* twenty cent piece, two silver *tostones,* four silver *pesos,* a ten *peso* bill, and half a pack of Monte Carlos.

"Tsk, tsk," clucks the *capitán,* pocketing the money. "This hardly pays for your night's lodging." He tosses me the half-pack of butts. "Keep these, you might need them."

I have counted on that. "Thanks," I say, slowly relaxing my tense belly muscles, "I *might.*"

It is beginning to be daylight as we step through the *portal* into the dusty road.

"Take good care of my friend," admonishes the *capitán* as we start off down the road that winds away through the spiney *huisaches* and cactus.

I am walking slightly in advance with Bartolo to my left and José to my right still shouldering their arms. As we round the first bend out of sight of the *carcel,* Bartolo says one word in Spanish, "Halt!"

I stiffen in my tracks. I haven't expected it so soon. If they pull the *ley de fugo* now I haven't got a chance. We're too close to the prison for me to make a getaway even if I can handle Bartolo and José. I hear the click of metal against metal like a cartridge slipping into the chamber. I steel myself not to turn. My leg muscles tense for a leap.

"Forward."

My heart drops back into its cavity. I breathe. I obey the command, moving forward through the hot dust with just a backward glance. I see they are carrying rifles "at trail" now with bayonets fixed. I'd heard the click of the metal as they fixed bayonets. I breathe a momentary sigh of relief.

We walk.

THE sun pokes a bloodshot eye over the Sierras. The *huisaches* and cactus thin out. *Maguey* plants plunge their broadswords at the sky on either side of the road. Here is one with the pale yellow heart removed so that the *agua miel* may flow down and fill the cavity. *Pulque!*

We walk.

At each step our feet send up a puff of dust like the smoke from a rifle barrel. I stop and turn around. They grasp their guns with both hands, bayonets fixed toward me. Their faces are solemn and expressionless. I take the Monte Carlos from my shirt pocket.

"*Cigarro?*" I offer them the package.

They look at me and say nothing. I take out a butt and light it. Marijuana wasted.

"I know the governor," I say.

Bartolo looks at me and says nothing. José looks at me and says nothing. I continue smoking.

"It's worth a thousand *pesos* to me to see the governor."

From above comes the roar of a buzz saw. A plane wings out of a cloudbank going south for Oacala where the gover-

With my right shoe I smack Jose's mug.
The red pepper flies out, choking him.

nor's soldiers are behind in their pay, where the Agressores would like to get control of the silver mines by putting in their own governor.

"There he is," says Bartolo, pointing upward. "Get your thousand *pesos* ready."

I breathe a sigh of relief and grin. "But I can't see him up there."

José smirks. "He'll be down here in a minute."

Sure enough, right then a pursuit plane swoops out of the cloud bank on the tail of the unsuspecting jenny. There is a brief burst of fire from a machine gun. The jenny, which obviously is not armed, tries to maneuver and get away but sees the hopelessness of it and noses down for a landing. The other one is right on its tail. They land over toward the prison at Temiltepan out of my field of vision. I hear another burst of machine gun fire. I pray they didn't kill the governor.

JUST then a mule comes around the bend in the road ahead of us. An oak keg is strapped to each side of his wooden saddle. Behind him plods a little Tlachiquero dressed in the typical dirty white pyjama-like costume of the Indians. He wears a huge sombrero and carries a gourd as large as a Texas watermelon. Now and then he pokes the mule with a sharp stick to hurry him. I get an idea.

I say, "Would you turn your backs and let me run for it for a thousand pesos apiece?"

"*Seguro! Seguro!*" They both agree too readily.

The mule reaches a *maguey* with the heart cut out and stops to nibble the dry grass by the roadside. The Tlachiquero sticks the pointed end of the big gourd into the white cavity of the maguey filled with *agua miel*, places his mouth against a small hole cut in the top of the gourd and starts to suck.

I say, "It's a bargain." I bend over to untie my right shoe. I grin. "Don't you boys ever look in shoes for money?" I straighten up with the shoe in my right hand. I probe in it with my left. Bartolo and José crowd forward greedily. My left hand comes out full of the pulverized *chiles rojas*. I let Bartolo have it right in that sour puss of his.

With my right I smack the shoe into José's melancholy mugg. The rest of the red pepper flies out and, in a second, they are both bouncing around screaming with the pain in their eyes. I grab their rifles from where they have fallen and look to see what effect the mélee is having on the Tlachiquero. He is draining the filled gourd into one of the kegs, going about his business as if he is deaf and dumb.

I dash over behind a big *maguey* and ditch the rifles and then I rush back to the two *soldados* writhing in the dust of the road. I look for something to tie and gag them with. I feel a touch on the elbow. I look around.

The Tlachiquero is holding a *riata* of *henniquin* fiber and two red bandana handkerchiefs. "For the executioners," he says in Spig.

When something like that happens in my business, I don't ask questions. I take the help and thank Lady Luck and Old Hardhead.

After we've got them trussed, gagged, and moved far enough off the road that they won't be discovered for a couple of hours I say, "When I used that pepper I intended to *take* your mule, *compadre*. But since you've been so accommodating I'll ask you if I can borrow it."

For answer the Tlachiquero goes over to the mule, lifts down the two kegs, which now appear to be empty, unties a bundle of clothing from the wooden saddle, and steps over behind the nearest *maguey*.

He says, with a little tremor in his voice, "Everything I have is *yours, señor.*"

Curiously I watch him through the spears of *maguey* as he slips off the dirty pyjama-like shirt. I gasp. Two luscious, pale gold breasts lift their proud roundness to the sun. They move in delicate rhythm as the arms are lifted to remove the sombrero and shake out the dusky cascade of glinting hair. Then the hands begin to untie the cord that holds up the soiled white trousers. I try to turn my eyes away. My head won't budge.

The cord comes untied.

I suck in my belly. I let it out again slowly. Never have I seen such beautiful, delicately curved, succulent hips. They melt away into thighs whose curves are only thinly disguised by a cloud of pale silk. My mouth fills with saliva. I sweat.

"Morenita," I whisper huskily, and then she is beside me.

She throws her arms around my neck and presses her hot, pulsing body against me. I feel the quivering of her taut figure. Her warm breath is in my nostrils. I slip my mouth over her lips in a gesture of complete possession. I feel the darting fire of her ardor. After a little she speaks.

"I was afraid I wouldn't get back

from Temiltepan in time. . . . Oh, Sangre, I do love you so!"

"Did you deliver my message?"

"Yes. The peon in the pink blouse sent an answer. He said, 'Tell Blood his leg is ready to kill a hundred rats.' "

I pull her against me again as I say, "I hate to leave you, Morenita. But I've got to take the mule and go like hell."

"But where will Morenita see Blood Brown again?"

"In jail."

"Oh. . . . *No!*"

"In jail in Temiltepan."

I STRUM the aged guitar. The clack of my peg leg keeps time against the pavement. I sing.

> *"La Cucuracha . . . La Cu-u-u-*
> *Carachaaaaaa. . . .*
> *Ya no puede caminar. . . ."*

I can see the sentries on either side of the prison *portál* grinning at me. That's a good start, considering that I'm no expert on the guitar.

> *"Porque no tiene . . . Porque le*
> *falta-a-a. . . .*
> *Marijuana . . . Que . . . Fumar-r..."*

My right knee hurts like the devil where it fits into the drum-like socket of the peg leg. My ankle, calf, and foot are absolutely numb from being strapped so tightly against the back of my thigh. But my dirty red *serape* is long enough to hide the bulge of my foot at the rear. I doubt if even the *capitán* would recognize me in this get up. I'm a little awkward using a peg leg seeing how this is the first time I've ever worn one. I strum. I sing.

> "The Cockroach . . . The Cockroach. . . .

Now he can not take a walk. . . .
Because there is no . . . Because
    he has no
Marijuana . . . for a smoke. . . ."

My peg leg slips as I step up onto the curb and I fall on my back in the gutter. I grit my teeth at the pain in my doubled under foot. I grin as one of the sentries helps me up. I give him the sign of the Agressores.

His face sobers. "How did you lose your leg, comrad?"

I grin. "I kicked the governor and it broke off."

The two sentries laugh uproariously. An officer appears in the *portál*. The sentries sober, stiffen to attention, and present arms. The major glares at me.

"*Que pasa?*"

I strum and sing my parody.

> "El Gobernador . . . The Governor. . . .
> He would like to take a ride.
> The 'officero' says, 'como no?'
> He can take a ride inside."

The major's frown slowly turns to a smile.

" '*Sta bueno,*" he says. "But why do you malign the governor, *trobador?*"

I contort my face. "I hate the *gobernador*. He is a thieving capitalist. He is an oppressor of the common people. He is an Hacendado." I make the sign of the Aggressores.

"Ahh," smiles the major, "perhaps you would like to sing your little parody to the *gobernador* himself."

I hesitate as if in doubt.

"While," continues the major, "he take the ride."

I grin. "I will sing as I have never sung before."

I CLUMP after him with my guitar through the flag-stoned corridor into the gigantic square patio around which the prison is built. As we reach the patio the major flings an order over his shoulder.

"Cierre el portál!"

I hear the iron gates clang together. My stomach sinks down till it rubs against my pelvis. I haven't counted on their closing the *portál*. I look back in time to see a big black limousine draw up to the curb across the street. Do I see a flash of pink behind the wheel?"

I clack after the major. To my left across the patio I can see a blank adobe wall. It is pitted with little holes. We pass the fountain in the center of the patio and across to the iron barred door on the other side. The sentry standing in front of it salutes and steps to the right. We enter.

The room is dusky. On a bench in the center of it sits a little man with a pointed gray beard. His forehead and temples are beaded with sweat, his cheeks splotched with blood. One arm dangles limply against the edge of the bench. The other is twisted up behind his back and held there by a big powerful man with bushy red mustachios. The big man is too big for a Mex and too fair. I scent Russia in his heavy features.

He is speaking in guttural, stilted Spanish to the little man with the pointed gray beard.

"Do you tell us where the money is, Esperanza, or do I break your pretty arm?"

The major says, "Relax, Gakov, we're going to have a little entertainment. . . ."

"What?" growls Gakov.

"At the *gobernador's* expense." The major winks at Gakov.

Gakov says, "Ohhhhh," stretches his heavy-lipped mouth into a horrible grin, and releases the twisted arm.

The major turns to me, *"Empiece, trobador!"*

The governor shakes the sweat from his bloodshot eyes and looks up at me as if to say, "What new torment is this?"

I begin strumming. I sing the parody. Gakov and the major laugh heartily. I make up another parody. They laugh again. The governor just sits and looks through me as if I'm not here. Gakov, exhilarated by the music, suddenly leaps at Esperanza again and twists the little man's arm until I hear the bones begin to pop. The governor writhes with the pain and finally gasps, "I'll tell! I'll tell!"

I look over my shoulder to see if the sentry is looking through the door. He isn't. I stick my right hand into the sounding box of the guitar and grasp the handle of my automatic. I jerk it out quickly, ripping off the strings.

"No you don't tell, governor," I say in a low voice. "Hold it, major! I don't want to kill anybody but I mean to get the governor out of here."

"Yiiaaaaggghh!" hisses Gakov, quivering with rage.

"Fool!" says the major. "I've only to call the sentry and you're a dead man."

"You've only to call the sentry and *you're* a dead man. Come on, Esperanza, take the major's Luger."

The governor almost sobs. He tries to lift his helpless dangling arms. "I can't."

"O. K. I'll do it. You try to make the door without alarming the sentry." I cross to the major and with a quick movement remove his Luger from the brown leather holster.

THE governor walks quietly past me toward the barred door. Keeping

Through the *maguey* I watch the young man disrobe, and—*carramba!*—it is no man!

Gakov and the major covered with the two gats, I back toward him. I whisper over my shoulder.

"Lift the latch with your knee. It isn't locked. Pull the door open with your foot, then step aside so I can get through first to cover the sentry."

Esperanza manages the door without a sound. I back softly through it, remembering that the sentry had stepped to the right of the doorway as we went in.

I leap backward one step to cover him. He isn't there. Lightning strikes the back of my head. The day turns pitch black.

I'm swimming. A bright red fish dashes past in front of my eyes. I gulp. A river of water rushes into my lungs. I sputter and gasp. Then somebody jerks my head out of the fountain. Somebody laughs. I turn my aching eyes. It is the major. Behind him is a squad of *sol-dados*. I try to grin. I look for the governor. Just then Gakov appears roughly dragging Esperanza after him.

"I did it!" he shouts. "The bills are hidden in the tires."

The little governor just stands there, looking helplessly at me, his glazed eyes almost closed. His shoulders sag as much as to say, "I'm sorry, but I couldn't stand the pain any longer. I had to tell."

The major laughs heartily. "Pretty smart. Stay here, Gakov, the money won't walk away. Let's take care of our friends first. It's been so nice to have them with us. And we probably won't see them again."

Gakov roars with laughter. "So we won't, major. So we won't."

The major gives a sharp command. The squad divides ranks. The governor steps into place and I behind him. We start marching across the square patio to the blank adobe wall that is pitted with little holes. My peg leg makes an odd hollow sound on the flagstones of the patio.

We are almost to the wall. The major shouts. We halt. The squad about faces and returns ten paces. They stand with their backs to us as the major inspects rifles. He gives another order. They about face and stand at attention.

The major approaches us with two handkerchiefs. There is something like a sneer on his face. The governor waves the handkerchief away. The major steps up to me.

I say, "If the smoke don't get in your eyes, major, it certainly don't get in mine."

He grins wryly.

The governor says, "On what grounds will you explain this execution to the *presidente?*"

"The only grounds one has in Mexico. The *ley de fugo.*"

I say, "Political prisoners trying to escape. But *you* can't shoot me, major."

He looks at me peculiarly. "My soldiers can." The major walks away and shouts, *"Listo!"* The *soldados* leap to attention.

I say, "Nothing but a silver bullet will kill Sangre Brown."

The major gasps. "Sangre Brown? Are you Sangre Brown?" He bellows, *"Armas arriba!!"* The squad raises their rifles to take aim.

"Too late, major," I say, sliding down to a sitting posture with my peg leg propped up on my left knee. My right hand slips quickly into the drum-like

socket. I squeeze the trigger. A stream of lead pours out of the Thompson in my peg leg and the line of *soldados* keels over like a row of dominoes.

WITH the most idiotic look on his face the major bellows, *"Fire!"*

I say, "Did I fire too soon, major? I am sorry."

The major screams, *"Santa Carissima!* This cannot be. This is without precedent. The prisoners have executed the firing squad!"

"Calm yourself, major. Remove your Luger, once again, from the holster and toss it to me. Be *careful*, major. I don't want to shoot an officer. That's right. Now come here, major. You walk in front of the governor and myself. Come on, governor. Let's go. One, two. One, two. . . . One, two."

I can see a confused group of soldiers looking in through the iron bars of the closed gate. I look for Gakov. He is not in sight.

"The little round hard thing that is hurting your back, major, is the barrel of your Luger. If we don't get through this *portál* you'll go through the *portál* of Paradise. By the way, major, where is Gakov?"

"Isn't he here?" The major takes a quick look around. "The dirty *ladron!* He has sneaked off to get the hundred thousand!" Then, suddenly he laughs. "Well, at least *you* won't get that and without the money Esperanza hasn't a chance to keep control of Oacala."

We arrive at the *portál*. A group of *soldados* are standing outside with ominous-looking rifles. The black limousine is gone from the curb. I begin to wonder what my next move is going to be. I jab the Luger a little harder into the major's back.

I whisper, "Shall I mow them down

with the Thompson, major, or will you give orders?"

"*Abre el portal! . . . Abre el portal!!*"

AFTER much suspicious muttering one of the *soldados* produces a large iron key and unlocks the metal gates. Just as they swing back, Gakov crashes through the group of soldiers from the street. He is streaming with sweat. His eyes are bloodshot. He is breathing heavily. He shouts at the major without even seeming to see us.

"I have been to the plane. The money is not there. The tires have been stolen from the landing gear!"

Out of the corner of my eye I see the black limousine coming down the street. I jab the Luger even harder into the major's back.

I say, "Out of the way, Gakov!"

He says, "*Carambissimo!* It is the peg-leg!" He shouts to the soldiers behind him. "Shoot him. Bayonet him! *Kill him!*"

The black limousine stops across the street. I hate to do it but I have to. I lift my peg leg and let him have it. The force of the slugs in his belly knocks Gakov backward onto the edge of the curb. He takes two *soldados* with him. With a horrible gurgle he rolls off into the gutter and lies still. For a second nobody moves. Nobody makes a sound. I can feel the major quivering with fear at the end of the Luger.

I say, "Drop your rifles and run, you Brown Bellies, or I'll give you the same."

Instantly there is a tremendous clatter of metal against pavement and flying legs disappear in all directions. I can see a peon in a pink blouse sitting behind the wheel of the black limousine.

"Proceed, major." We reach the center of the street. "Right face, major. Now, walk straight up the center of the

street until you reach the corner if you don't want any holes in your nice new uniform.

The major begins walking, very fast. The peon opens the front door.

I say, "Get in, governor," and opening the rear door leap in, slamming it after me. "Good work, Number Nineteen." The car lurches forward.

"Thanks, where to?" says Nineteen in Mex.

"The plane. We've got to find those tires for the governor."

"They're here," says a meek voice beside me, "in the trunk on the rear."

I'm a son of a gunman if it isn't Morenita. She's dressed like she was the day I slugged the *soldados* of the *capitán.*

"Go like hell for Oacala. Where the devil?" I begin. She falls across my lap, her arms around my neck. Something soft and damp and quivering closes over my mouth. A flick of red flame sears my tingling lips. Her firm round breasts are pressed against my chest. A vague woman fragrance makes me draw my breath in sharply. Morenita moves her wet lips from my mouth to my ear.

She whispers, "You say you be in jail at Temiltepan . . . so-o . . . I go back to see pink blouse. We arrive at the *portál.* We hear Gakov say the money is in the tires. We take off the tires and set fire to both planes so we cannot be follow."

I grin. I can feel her small hands caressing my back. One of them encounters my doubled under foot. She says, "Oh, your poor leg!" and sits up suddenly. With deft movements she unstraps my ankle from my thigh, the touch of her hand on my flesh sending thrills across the small of my back. She loosens the strap that holds the peg leg

(Continued on page 124)

DRUMS OF DOOM

[Continued from page 85]

The pressure against his hand increased. Beneath her thin summery dress he felt the burning softness of her body, and his blood came quicker. Smiling, he turned to draw her to him. "Johnny, Johnny!" she laughed, "we'll be arrested if we keep this up. Come on, let's go down and visit that Fort Marion. Maybe you'll see some of your precious ghosts there."

IT WAS blazing hot in the courtyard of Fort Marion when they entered through the main gate over the drawbridge.

In one corner of the stone court an American Legion drum and bugle corps were blaring away with a great flourish. John Lavery recalled it was Independence Day. He glanced idly around.

The fort teemed with people, gayly attired in holiday dress, but Lavery did not appear to see them. Instead, his dark puzzled eyes roved over the ancient battlements as though searching for something. The strange obsession that had gripped him when he had first arrived in St. Augustine was growing stronger. He felt vaguely uneasy, as though he faced some unknown danger.

A crinkled, sun-tanned guide approached them, handed Lavery a pamphlet. "Fort Marion," he began in a monotonous sing-sing voice, "was built in 1603, although it was then called San Marco. It replaced the old Spanish fort ravaged by the English in 1586. Although rebuilt again at a later period, much of the original stone of Fort San Marco is still here. Would you care to visit the prison dungeons?"

An inexplicable wave of dread swept over Lavery. He shook his head slowly. "Thanks—we'll just ramble around ourselves—"

The guide left them and Lavery steered Doris away from the teeming crowds. They found a dark, cool passageway and entered it.

In here the walls were moist, and heavy with the moss of centuries. A quiet vast brooding lay over the place— a silence that reeked of things long dead and forgotten. Lavery was restive. He shuffled through the passageway, his eyes probing the shadows, seeming to see ghostly shapes ahead; to hear whisperings in the dusky air about him.

SOMETHING was happening to him —something weird, inexplicable. He shook himself, strove to thrust off the spell, found it impossible. In some mad way he was losing his memory. When he had stepped into that dark, dank corridor from the hot courtyard, he had left behind the present. He had a strange feeling he was wandering back through the misty centuries, groping blindly for something he felt he would find there.

It was Doris who discovered three moss-covered steps that led down to a dungeon. Her excited voice smashed the brooding silence, seemed a sacrilege in that place. "John—let's see this. It looks so cool and dark down there."

It was dark. It was pitch black. The fort authorities supplied electric lighting for these horror holes, but in this case the bulb had burned out. But Lavery had no knowledge of that. To him, the utter darkness seemed fitting, proper —a tribute of black silence to the brooding ghosts that must be there.

"For a Spaniard, thou art indeed beautiful," he said.

Within the dungeon he felt the warm, curving body of his wife snuggle tight against him. Two cool arms stole about his neck, pulled his head down.

"John," she whispered, "Aren't you going to take advantage of the darkness?"

He shuddered. Then his strong arms went around her waist, pulled her to him. Her moist, quivering lips sought his, found them. As he pressed her yielding body ever closer, the warmth of her breath on his mouth nearly drove him mad. He became more possessive almost savage. But no matter how roughly he held her she uttered no protest.

Her breath was a half-sob . . . a moan of pleasure. . . .

THEN abruptly, drifting through the massive stone walls came a faint booming of drums. John Lavery stiffened, pushed Doris roughly from him. Desire fled from his veins, died completely.

The American Legion corps—the bugle and drum corps of course! Remembering them he tried to smile, to shake off the sudden dread that assailed him. He failed.

He stood in the darkness, fists clenched, the nails ripping his palms, his eyes glaring, while the dull boom of drums thudded into his soul.

Something was happening to him—something weird, terrible. Perhaps he was going mad. Those drums outside —they were driving him crazy!

His hoarse labored breathing told Doris something was wrong. Crowding close, she slid her arms about his shoulders. "John," came her anxious whisper, "What's happened?"

Lavery did not reply. Somehow his very identity was slipping from him. The name "John" rang unfamiliar in his ears. It was not his name. She should call him by his right name—but what was it? He realized he had forgotten that too!

Trembling, he brushed his hand across his forehead, found it dripping with cold sweat. "This dungeon," he muttered thickly. *"I've been here before!"*

"Here—before?" Her voice rose, startled. "What are you talking about John? That's impossible! You said you'd never been to Florida in your life. That's why—".

His hand shot out, gripped her by the shoulder: "Silence!" Fumbling in his pockets he produced a match lighted it. "The cross!" he muttered hoarsely, "The cross carved in the wall! I know I have been here before. This will prove it!"

HE DROPPED to his knees and in the tiny flare cast by the match feverishly scanned the walls. At last a low growl of triumph. "The cross! There it is!"

Bewildered, Doris' eyes followed his pointing hand, saw carved in the ancient stone a faint semblance of a cross. Her lips twisted strangely. Panic was in her voice when she asked: "How—how— did you know?"

Desperately, furiously he battled to remember, while silence hung oppressive in the dungeon. Lavery was no longer Lavery. He was some one else, a man unnamed, a man who had perished there centuries ago.

The drums in the courtyard were pounding again. They were not American Legion drums, but drums of doom, whose echo came rumbling out of a long dead past. Lavery stretched out his hand, closed it over the girl's arm. She cried out in sudden pain. He staggered back, gasped and a great light burst in his eyes. "Dolores! Judas!" he shouted. "Betrayer! Feel thou my vengeance!"

Too late the girl realized she was trapped. His strong fingers were at her soft throat, digging in mercilessly. She tried to scream, but no sound came from her lips.

Lavery forced her back, savagely, bitterly. In him was a flaming, overpowering lust for revenge, a heritage handed down over a space of two hundred and fifty years.

Grimly, inexorably he finished his task. When he rose to his feet swaying, Doris, his Spanish wife, lay dead. Numbly, with mind reeling, Lavery stumbled from the dungeon and staggered through the dark passageway.

He had a strange impression that a ghost walked at his side—the ghost of a grim, smiling, swashbuckling, dangerous cavalier. A ghost that smiled on him and whispered: "Juan, Juan, my son. Long have I waited for thee to meet the Spanish temptress. . . ."

HE CAME out in the blazing hot courtyard before a crowd of people. The crinkled, sun-tanned guide was leading them about, explaining things as he went. Haggard and white of face John Lavery stumbled up to him, said: "You'd better call the police. I have just killed my wife."

The Woman of Cayenne

[Continued from page 27]

Suddenly he began to laugh. The irony of it would not admit a tragic attitude. Young Collins betrayed by this girl now offering herself to him, and Pieters, just a coarse beast of the clay, but guiltless, because he had acted only according to his own nature.

"You can pull up your dress, Geneste," said Neale. "I'm through with you."

Big Pieters roared with laughter. "You have one on the house before you go, hey, sailor?" he cried.

Neale shook his head and turned away. He went out through the crowded bar-room into the silent street. Little Collins, the Kansas boy, buried under the jungle mud, and that woman in the little room!

He didn't exonerate himself. He knew it was true what Geneste had said. If he had taken her, and violated his sense of honor to his friend, there would have been no Pieters, no drab bar-room lovers.

That was the difficulty about life for the Tumbleweed; when you tried to do right, you generally went wrong. But there would be no exalted sense of honor in his future dealings with his kind.

"I'm drunk," thought Neale.

"You come with me, sailor! Ah, I see you before. You have no money, *chéri*, and you have been sick. Come with me!"

The Tumbleweed looked at the slender brown girl before him, and his heart quickened. One must go down into the mud in order to arise. In future he would be a very different Tumbleweed, but to-night—to-night, heartsick as he was . . . .

She linked his arm through hers and pressed her curving breast against his arm, and Neale went with her.

Thieves' Justice

[Continued from page 93]

seen a man whom she could not influence. Surely this wizened little Mexican would prove no exception.

They rested together, the lady and Juan, one afternoon beneath the trees beside the stream. He squatted on his haunches smoking a brown paper cigarette while she lay stretched full length on the green carpet of jungle grass. Her skirt gaped open revealing white flesh, her riding breeches were tightly pressed about her full hips. She sat up suddenly and wrote:

"I am hot. Is there a pool where I can bathe?"

Juan grinned. "*Si, señora,* I will show you!" He handed her the answer, led the way.

Ten minutes later she lowered her white body into the icy coldness of the mountain stream. In the distance, his head turned discreetly away, old Juan squatted on the bank smoking his interminable cigarettes. Presently she clambered from the pool, flexed her muscles serenely, hoping that the white gleam of her dripping body in the sunlight would attract the old man's eyes. He did not turn.

It was the work of a moment to step

into brief panties, sheer and thin, to run toward his crouching figure. She crashed relentlessly through the underbrush before he saw her. Her face was contorted with seeming fright, she threw her trembling body into his protective arms pointing back the way she had come. For a moment he held her close while she shivered against him, then suddenly a knife appeared as if by magic in his hand. He pushed her aside, ran to search for the thing that had frightened her.

Promptly she relaxed with a look of cunning, lay down on the sod as if she had fainted. Moments later she heard his approach but kept her eyes tightly closed. She knew that her long lashes were like the shadowed wings of birds, her breasts were twin mounds, moving as she breathed. She knew he stood beside her, knew when he knelt, felt his breath on her throat. The gentle touch of his fingers on her bare flesh, the sobbing catch in his breathing. She opened her eyes. For a second he drew back, but she pulled him nearer until his head rested on the softness of her white shoulder, his lips buried in the warm hollows of her throat.

Long moments later she wrote on the little pad: "Do you love me, Juan?"

His brown eyes were those of an uncertain dog, full of misery. She knew she had won, knew if this wizened old man did have money her chances of getting it were much better than those of her husband and his mistress. The gnarled fingers went painfully across the little pad in answer to her question.

"*Si, señora, por Dios!*"

Yes, God help me! Poor Juan was beginning to doubt his own destiny.

TWO nights later Juan rose in the middle of the night and stole out of the house. Cuca, restless and alert, ran for the *patio* of Curtis' place. Soon Curtis, too, came from his couch, met his mistress, and headed up the mountain trail after the deaf and dumb man. Impatiently Cuca awaited his return.

Lorraine, secure in her room slept on. She did not hear the prowler that entered to make off with Jim Curtis' hat and coat. Yet she thought nothing of Curtis' absence the next morning as he often rode early to Balsas to inaugurate a three or four day spree.

The same morning Cuca awakened to find her husband beside her, the three neat stacks of silver pesos atop the bureau with the stained machet. But there was no ear! Thank God for that! Even when Lorraine told her that Curtis had departed for Balsas she did not worry. Perhaps Curtis had found the money and had taken it to Balsas for safety. Even now he might be arranging for their flight.

Old Juan rode to Mamasita's as usual, his silver pesos clanking in his shirt front. He gave a *muchacho* two pesos, wrote him a note and sent him on his way. Then he sat down to drink his *tequila* and wait.

A FEW hours later a man clattered up the street of the town attired like a dandy of the ranches. His sombrero was the broadest, his silver spurs the longest. A quirt hung from his wrist and silver dollars decorated his velvet jacket. Behind him clattered eight men, all well mounted, all savage looking fellows, bedecked with many colors.

They drew up before Mamasita's *cantina*, and the leader shouted, "Hola! Come out, old woman! Don Señor Pedro Bravo Gonzales de Romero y Mendias calls!'

He caught her angrily and the table fell.

Mamasita Diega bustled out at the sound of that glorious name, for Don Pedro owned the biggest ranch, the richest *hacienda* in the entire state. Bowing and scraping profusely Mamasita stood in the dust of the roadway waiting the pleasure of the great men.

"My friend, Juan Garcia," roared Don Pedro, "he awaits me here?"

Mamasita could scarcely believe her ears but somehow, someway, with the aid of an open-mouthed servant they aroused Juan Garcia from his sleep in the corner, got him into the street. Don Pedro embraced him like a brother, while his men gathered around talking and chatting. Mamasita was forced to bring out many bottles of *tequila* before they rode away, Juan sitting proudly on his grey mule.

Cuca was surprised. To have an unexpected guest was unusual; to have nine was too much. She protested volubly but beneath the admiring gaze of Don Pedro she blossomed like a rose and fixed them all a wonderful meal.

Later that night they all rode away, but Juan locked Cuca firmly in her room.

Horses were left in a little glade, and the men made trip after trip to the mountainside led by the skinny Juan. From the mountainside they carried their burdens to the little smelter belonging to the mine. A few hours later when the awakened workers, the miners themselves, came to see what was the clatter, they found the smelter in full blast, with grinning, wild-looking fellows standing guard at the doorway while their companions worked over the small furnace. Wisely the peons went back to bed.

Lorraine paid no attention. Her husband ran the mine, his foreman during his absence. Naturally she thought the foreman was in charge. Instead of which he was drinking jovially with Don Pedro and the mute, Juan, all during the night.

Into the afternoon of the second day the work continued, the smelter being taken over by Don Pedro himself. He sent a man into the village for *tequila* and treated the idle peons to drink in profusion.

After dinner Juan drew Cuca aside. He wrote on his pad:

"I am going away with Don Pedro tonight. We go to his *hacienda.* You can stay here or go back to your mother."

She made sounds of loud crying, great grief, seized his pad and wrote: "I have been a good wife to you, Juan. Why do you desert me, penniless, with no money?"

Juan read and answered: "I will leave you with a nice present. Meet me tonight at the glade above the bridge."

Cuca's heart bounded. He was going to give her part of his treasure! At least show her where it was concealed! Well, it was good to be rid of the old fool. When Curtis returned, they could go away together, take the money, leave the *gringo* woman and go to Mexico City.

WHEN Juan told Lorraine of his departure she cried in his skinny arms, begged him to take her with him. The old fool! After all she had given him, to desert her without a peso!

"At least," she wrote, "leave me some money so that I can go away from this man I hate."

He nodded eagerly, caressed her. He wrote, "I will leave you with a nice present, *corazon.* Meet me in two hours at the glade above the bridge!" He kissed her passionately—and left.

Two hours later.

Softly Lorraine crept over the bridge above the roaring stream. The old fool was going to show her his cache! She had to laugh at how easy it had been. When Jim Curtis came back from his binge, he wouldn't find *her* there! She'd take the old fool's money and get clear out of the country. How much, she pondered, would it be? If it was really part of Zapata's treasure, the amount would be limitless! What—?

She almost stumbled over Cuca who sat in a shadow her back against a rock. The Mexican girl sprang to her feet. The *gringo* woman drew back, startled.

"What are *you* doing here?" they said together.

There might have been some trouble, some lying explanations from both if the clatter of hooves on the bridge had not interrupted. Into the moonlight glade trotted the gaunt, grey mule of Juan

Garcia, who smiled down at the women. A heavy package was tied to the pommel of his saddle, his spurs glinted as he dismounted. Don Pedro clattered to a halt behind his friend. Juan's sombrero swept low, he bowed from the waist.

"*Buenas noches, señoras,*" he said and stood grinning at them.

Don Pedro roared with laughter from the back of his mount.

"You speak," gasped Cuca! "What miracle is this? You speak? You hear?"

"Perfectly," said Juan, grinning like a wolf. "I speak well and I hear too well!"

Lorraine stood still, said nothing, but Cuca became almost hysterical. "Liar! Thief! Murderer! *Bandido!* For seven years you say nothing, you pretend to be deaf! And now you speak, now you hear. All that time you played a game!"

JUAN spoke to Lorraine, disregarding his wife. His voice was almost soft, almost tender. "Excuse me, please, if I do this thing to you. As she says, for seven years I have played a deaf mute, pretending neither to hear nor to speak. Just as you have heard, I did ride with Zapata years ago! I am not ashamed and I have nothing to lose now! I had some silver—that same silver which attracted your cupidity. Now I will not have to worry about it any longer because last night we borrowed your husband's smelter and converted it into ingots, which my very good friend Don Pedro is buying from me. His word will not be questioned, so there is no need for me to go on with my deception!"

"Thief! *Bandido!* Murderer!" screamed Cuca. "What have you done with Jose? What have you done with Señor Curtis?"

"I?" Juan's voice was suave. "Oh,

you mean what have I done with your lovers? Ah, Cuca, and you Lorraine, how I sigh for faithless women! But let us speak no more, I must ride with my friend.'

He reached up, lifted the heavy package from his saddle and tossed it at the feet of the two women. "A present for you, my friends," he said softly, and sprang to the mule's back. Together the women snatched at the package, pulled aside the strings, tore off the cloth coverings.

The severed heads of Jose, the betrayer, and Curtis, the Judas, rolled into the moonlight, white eyeballs gleaming and glittering malevolently.

Lorraine sank to her knees, retched, her face ghastly white.

But Cuca screamed, "Murderer! Killer! *Bandido,* you will pay for this!"

"Me?" said Juan. "*I* pay for this? I know nothing of it! My friend Don Pedro found the package on the trail as he rode from the town. Surely no one will doubt the word of Don Señor Pedro Bravo Gonzales de Romero y Mendias! And if they should, mind you, I say if they should, be careful! Juan Guedea, the right hand of Zapata, may yet ride again! That *bandido* is terrible in his wrath, you may well believe!"

They wheeled, clattered across the bridge. Other hoof beats sounded in the distance and back into the moonlit glade floated a song:

"*La Cucaracha, La Cucaracha,*
Ya no puede caminar."

Eventually, the words of the bandit song and the wind-borne sound of much laughter. Now the only sound in the glade was the bubbling roar of the river and the rhythmic sobbing of two frightened, faithless women.

HUMP OF SERRANO

{Continued from page 15}

Behind the tree the quaking lieutenant tensed, raised the gun. The humpback stepped on the board porch, made for the door. Just as he reached it, it swung open. A short pace inside the room stood Conchita, her lips twisted, her eyes burning madly. She peered at the newcomer who said a short word. The woman's hand flew to her mouth.

"No," she screamed, "it is not—"

It was too late. The praying lieutenant pulled the trigger, the bullet sped toward the man's humped back.

too late. A slug from the Kid's gold mounted gun caught him behind the ear, knocked him three feet into the ditch where he lay still.

The Sabinas Kid stepped over the seat back, pushed the girl aside and slid the car into gear. Behind them the sky was red with the flame of the burning cottage.

"The buzzards are gone," he said softly and laughed. "They'll sell no more of their damned white powder! We are both avenged."

Next Month—

Lew Merrill Writes of Romance In a Convict Camp—
Love Annealed With Blood. Don't Miss—

FOREST FURY

A great roar filled the air, a sheet of flame sprang up. The whole cottage rocked, collapsed like a house of cards. A hurtling board caught the lieutenant squarely between the eye, crashed through his skull and tore the top away as a gigantic sickle might. The woman and the humpback had strangely disappeared.

A HALF block down the road the car rocked as if shaken by an earthquake. Taylor scrambled out, ran a few steps down the road. "God," he muttered drunkenly, "what was that? Sounded like a ton of dynamite—" He whirled, gun in hand, but he, too, was

The girl shuddered. "What was it?" she whispered, awestricken at the havoc this man had wrought.

"Nitro," he laughed. "A tiny bottle of nitroglycerine! I put it in the hump of Serrano, packed shale and rocks about it. Someone fired into the hump!"

A mile farther on he stopped the car and alit. A horse nickered a welcome from the bushes. "Take me with you," the woman whispered. He leaned and kissed her lips, pressed her close. She strained to him, her eyes hot with passion, her breasts moving tremulously against him.

"No," he said, a strange light in his eyes, "I am a lone wolf. Perhaps some

» **IF YOU DO NOT ADD** **3 INCHES TO**
AT LEAST **YOUR CHEST**

... it won't cost you one cent!"— Signed: GEORGE F. JOWETT

THREE SOLID INCHES of muscles added to your chest and at least two inches added to each of your biceps, or it won't cost you a penny. I know what I am talking about ... I wouldn't dare make this startling agreement if I wasn't sure I could do it.

All I want is a chance to prove it! Those skinny fellows who are discouraged are the men I want to work with. I'll show them how to build a strong man's body... and do it quickly. And I don't mean cream-puff muscles either. Wouldn't you, too, like to get a he-man's chest like the idealized figure above? I will show you how to get real, genuine invincible muscles that will make your men friends respect you and women admire you!

So many of my pupils have gained

GEORGE F. JOWETT
"Champion of Champions"
Winner of many contests for strength and physical perfection!

tremendous development that I am willing to stake my reputation that you can do the same... *remember...if I fail it will cost you nothing!*

Nothing Can Take The Place of My Weight — Resistance Method With Progressive Dumbbells!

The Jowett System features the weight resistance method that has been tested and endorsed by many of the world's most famous strong men. By using this proven, scientific system of graduated weights, you can quickly develop your muscles and broaden your chest!

Send for "MOULDING A MIGHTY CHEST" A SPECIAL COURSE FOR ONLY 25c.

I will not limit you to the chest, develop any part or all of your body. Try any one of my test courses listed below at 25c. Or, try all six of them for only $1.00. You can't make a mistake. The assurance of the strongest armed man in the world stands behind these courses!

FREE BOOK WITH PHOTOS OF FAMOUS STRONG MEN!

RUSH THE COUPON TODAY AND I WILL INCLUDE A FREE COPY OF

"Nerves of Steel...Muscles Like Iron"

It is a priceless book to the strength fan and muscle builder. Full of pictures of marvelous bodied men who tell you decisively how you can build symmetry and strength the Jowett way! Reach out— Grasp this Special Offer.

JOWETT INSTITUTE of PHYSICAL CULTURE
Dept. 22Fd, 422 Poplar Street, Scranton, Pa.
Send by return mail, prepaid, the courses checked below, for which I am enclosing $........
☐ All 6 Books for $1.00
☐ Moulding a Mighty Arm, 25c ☐ Moulding a Mighty Chest, 25c
☐ Moulding a Mighty Back, 25c ☐ Moulding Mighty Legs, 25c
☐ Moulding a Mighty Grip, 25c ☐ Strong Man Stunts Made Easy 25c.

Name _____

Address _____

day, some place we meet. *Quien sabe?* But now the Sabinas Kid must ride alone. Now and, forever."

She sat silently behind the wheel until she heard the creak of saddle leather, the jingle of silver ornaments fading away in the distance. Slowly she turned the car about and headed for the bridge.

DEATH IN THE DESERT

[Continued from page 65]

Abd-el-Rahman had taken him on his journey toward Damascus.

Not a sound came from the heights; only the soaring vultures, strung out in a long line across the sky, were horribly significant. As Peter climbed, he could see the column of soldiers winding like a snake across the desert, while behind them stragglers dotted the desert. Higher and higher, for another hour, Peter ascended; then suddenly he came upon a tiny pool of water fed by a stream that gushed out of the rocks.

He dropped upon his face and drank feverishly, checking himself, then drinking again, laving his hands and face. He arose with a new feeling of strength in him. Again he climbed and climbed.

But the vultures were wheeling low above the face of the summit now, and dropping down behind the peak.

Higher still, and then suddenly the goat track yielded to the pass into the little valley where the Druse village was.

The stone huts were still standing, and at first sight it seemed that no one had come that way. But there was the body of a *légionnaire,* cloven almost in half by a Druse scimitar. And there were two more, and then a little huddle of white-clad forms in a pool of drying blood.

A vulture dropped silently beside it.

Peter ran forward, his heart thumping in his chest.

There was old Abd-el-Rahman, riddled with bullets, his hand still clutching his scimitar. And there were more Druses, and more. God, the body of a woman, hacked and mutilated; and another!

A woman was screaming somewhere in the village. Peter saw forms moving in the distance, but the sunlight dimmed his eyes.

A woman stirring feebly beside the track, half nude in the blazing sunlight— Fatima!

Peter stopped with a cry of horror. He dared not go on, dared not see what now he knew that he would have to see, beyond that pile of grisly corpses that had been mowed down by bullets, and blocked the way, a wall of dead flesh, four feet high.

"Fatima! Where is Koraida?"

PETER had spoken in Arabic, which Fatima did not understand. But she heard him, she understood her sister's name, she opened her eyes.

Frightfully gashed and ripped by bayonets, after the scum of the Legion had wrought their will upon her, it was a miracle that she was still conscious.

"Koraida?" Recognition came into her eyes. "Ah, it is you," she whispered in French. "You have come back to me, beloved?"

"Yes, yes," sobbed Peter. "I have come back for you, Fatima. But where is Koraida?"

She seemed to be struggling back from the verge of death. "Koraida? There, in

LOOK!

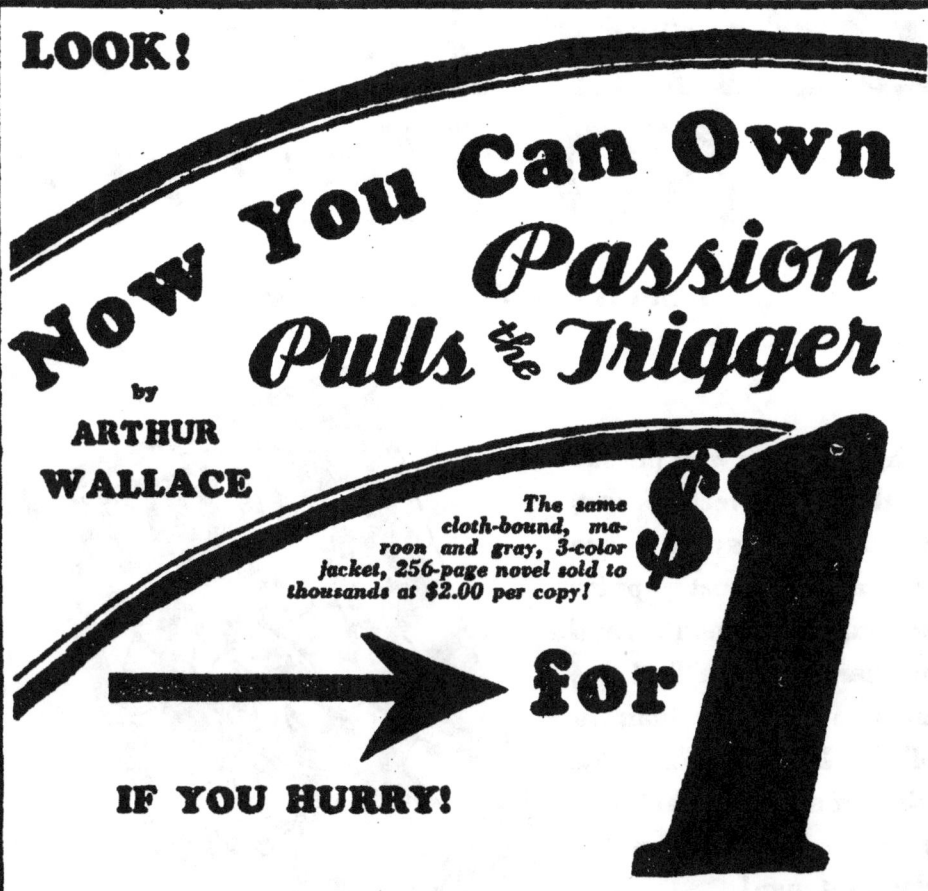

Now You Can Own *Passion Pulls the Trigger*

by ARTHUR WALLACE

The same cloth-bound, maroon and gray, 3-color jacket, 256-page novel sold to thousands at $2.00 per copy!

for $1

IF YOU HURRY!

How Can We Do It?

It's a simple problem in mathematics. Three months ago we announced that if 2000 readers would subscribe to this new author-owned book publishing plan, we could sell full-size, cloth-bound novels that book stores wouldn't handle, at the phenomenal price of $1.00. The response (at first) was slow. We were forced to raise the price to $2.00 per book. Then, out of a clear sky, orders came pouring in. Before we knew it the first edition was sold out and we were over the 2000 mark!

The Authors' Committee immediately ordered a second edition of PASSION PULLS THE TRIGGER. It is identical with the $2.00 book. There are 1500 copies ready to be shipped to you at $1.00 each. From now on all our books will be $1.00. Your response has made this possible.

Don't hesitate. PASSION PULLS THE TRIGGER is not a reprint nor a magazine. It's a hard cover book, each page of which will thrill you!

Orders can be accepted from the United States only since PASSION PULLS THE TRIGGER has been banned from Canada.

- -

Valhalla Press   A-6
210 Fifth Avenue
New York City

 I enclose $1.00 (Cash, check, m. o.—no C. O. D.). Send me, via fast Express, one copy of PASSION PULLS THE TRIGGER by Arthur Wallace.

Name_____ Age_____

Address_____ City_____ State_____

(We reserve the right to return your money if the edition of 1500 copies is exhausted prior to the receipt of your order.)

DEATH TAKES NO HOLIDAY

in SPICY DETECTIVE STORIES

—but the men who pursue death *do!* Detectives are, despite the way they are presented in most popular fiction, only human . . . and nowhere will you find this more e v i d e n t than in SPICY DETECTIVE. The wiles of a woman can hamper—or help—even the cleverest man!

Look for romance along with grim murder in these and other stories:

CAT'S PAW
by Mort Lansing

THE MILLION BUCK SNATCH
by Robert Leslie Bellem

SHARK KILL
by Thomas H. Byrnes

SPY BAIT
by Alan Anderson

You'll Find the June Issue of

SPICY DETECTIVE STORIES

On Sale April 25th

the house! There are some of the French dogs still here. Save her. And then come back to me, for I—love you—"

Her head fell back, a shiver passed over her, and she was gone. Even in that moment screams of women and the roar of bestial voices broke upon Peter's ears. He left the dead girl in the sun, climbed over the stiffening corpses, and ran on. As he ran, he heard himself shouting oaths, damning, horrible oaths that he remembered from vivid experiences of his boyhood. All the depths of his personality seemed to have been spewed up, and he was no longer Peter Strange, but a raging madman.

At his cries, a *légionnaire* came reeling out of the chief's house. The blue coat was unfastened, the chest beneath was like a hairy ape's. It was Luigi. He straightened himself as he saw Peter in his Druse attire, opened his mouth to yelp.

Peter shot him through the brain.

HE saw the Corsican's leering face change to a blood-spattered horror as the body came crashing down, dead before it hit the ground. He leaped across it and ran into the house of Abd-el-Rahman, into the long room. And the sight he saw there was something that Peter was going to remember until the last day of his life.

The floor was heaped with dead Druses, the rugs were soaked in blood, which had spread like a film everywhere across the stones. The curtains that shielded the harem had been torn down, and at the farther end half a dozen women and girls lay moaning, mutilated by these fiends. Four *légionnaires*, slipping in the blood, reeled, belched and roared.

A fifth appeared, dragging a shrieking girl out of the storehouse in which she had hidden herself.

It was Koraida. Almost every vestige of clothing had been torn from her by the brute who had found her, one hand clutched at one of the soft shoulders on which Peter had laid his head, the other held the girl around the waist. The soldier, an enormous man, lifted her, swung her, so that her dark hair fell like a curtain to the blood-stained floor.

"Here is the pick of them all, comrades, this little filly," shouted the man. "She is mine!"

It was Novotsky.

Peter's cry drowned the din, the yells and the moaning. He leaped forward like a maniac. Yet even in that instant he saw that he could not shoot Novotsky without hitting Koraida.

With which sanity came back to him. A sudden, cold certainty took possession of him as he drew a bead on one of the four other men and shot him through the heart.

And a second, before their shouts of warning changed to an understanding of the situation. And a third, through the belly changing him into a screaming, pain-racked thing.

Then Novotsky had flung down the girl, and he and the fourth soldier were upon Peter.

He fired into Novotsky's face, and found that his magazine was empty. He swung his arm in an arc and brought the pistol down upon the giant's forehead, hearing the bone crack beneath the blow. As Novotsky went down, the fifth man grappled with him.

The man was a German, like so many of the Legion, and a trained boxer, apparently, for he landed stunning blows, right and left, on Peter's face. But Peter's hands had closed about the man's throat, and he knew that even in unconsciousness he would never let go.

THE blood was streaming from his nose and lips, and those hammer blows were stunning him. But his hands closed and tightened, until suddenly the blows ceased to fall, and the man was gasping, squirming, struggling in Peter's grip. And Peter was forcing his head back with his right hand, while the left shifted toward the base of the skull—back, back, until the snap of the vertebra cracked through the room like a pistol-shot.

Peter let the body fall. He stood dazed for an instant. Then he saw Novotsky trying to rise to his feet. Beside him lay a rifle with the bayonet attached.

Peter picked up the weapon, stepped back, and ran the Russian through the bowels. He twisted it out, struck down the writhing, howling wretch with the butt end, and turned to where Koraida crouched in the corner.

When he spoke her name, he saw the madness go out of her eyes. He clasped her in his arms and carried her into the room that had been his.

At the end of an hour he had calmed her and brought her back to sanity. He stripped the garments from a murdered girl and clothed her. He went back into the long room, but it was a death-shambles, with Novotsky the only living thing in it, gasping and choking in his long death-agony, and pleading for release.

Peter left him and went back to Koraida. He sat down beside her and took her hand in his.

"You know that they are all dead?" he asked.

"Yes, lord, I know. And I wish to die too. Be merciful to me. It will be quick."

"I am going to take you away," said Peter, "across the border of Palestine. We can reach there by dawn, and there you will be safe. Will you come with me, Koraida?"

"With thee?" She looked at him incredulously. "Thou—lovest me?"

"Since we met upon the field of battle, little warrior, little love of mine. Come, for there is nothing we can do here. Hold my hand, close your eyes, and let me guide you, as I shall do all the rest of our days together."

And, hand in hand, they went out of the stone house together and set their faces southward.

EEL TRAP

[Continued from page 77]

"You fool!" Fournier sputtered. "I have no wife! Women may fall for you, Eel, but this time the woman who made love to you was nothing but an underpaid secretary of mine!"

"That is a pity," I sighed.

He laughed bitterly as he turned away from me. But then he turned back again and leered at me most triumphantly. "The girl who will be my wife," he sneered, "is the girl I sent to guide you to my apartment. Remember her, Eel? Regine is her name. She loves *me*, and you wouldn't stand one chance in a million with her!"

"That, too, is a pity," I said. "Yes, indeed, that is a pity. And now, gentlemen, I must be going. May you have better luck next time." And if Paul Fournier wondered why I was laughing so very softly to myself as I walked away from them, he did not say so.

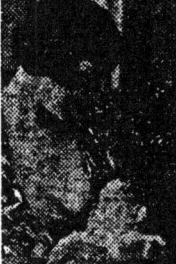

LATER, when my brave little launch had left the Yat Sun wharf far behind, my four trusted Malays went hard to work again, this time retriving the waterproof bales which they had previously lashed securely to the boat's keel. One or two of the bales, I noticed upon inspection, had suffered slight damage from their prolonged immersion, but it was of no consequence.

"We are not going to Selatpandjang," I said. "We are going instead to Bengkalis, where I know a man who will pay handsomely for the stuff we have here. Then you will each receive much money, and you will return to my good friend Lin Tsi, taking him a generous token of my appreciation."

In the cabin, my little Regine was waiting for me, and this time, upon entering, I closed the cabin door and locked it against intrusion. And having divested myself of wet outer garments, I sat beside Regine on the little couch there and drew her close to me. My lips found hers and my hands removed the heavy coat which I had draped about her to keep her warm.

"It will be a long journey to Bengkalis," I murmured, possessively embracing the warm, trembling body which quivered very promisingly against me. "We shall keep warm together, lest we both catch pneumonia."

And I thought of Paul Fournier, and smiled . . . .

BLOOD on the DOORSTEP

[Continued from page 105]

to my knee. It is heavy with the weight of the Thompson and drops to the floor. "Now, move your leg."

I try. The whole leg is absolutely numb from being strapped up so long.

"I can't." I take hold of my foot with both hands to ease it out straight but she brushes my hands aside, straightens my leg across her lap and, beginning at the ankle, starts massaging the numb flesh. Gradually, as her hands move upward, circulation is restored and I can feel the firm caressing pressure of her fingers.

The mercury rises in my spine. I stiffen. I am able to move my leg off her lap to the floor. She throws herself against me. I can see her breasts thrusting against the white silk blouse. I can feel her heart hammering against my chest. I am enveloped in a searing flame of ecstasy.

Vaguely I hear Number Nineteen say, "How do you feel, governor?"

"A little bruised, but thankful to be alive. Santa Maria! My neck is so stiff I cannot turn my head."

I hear Number Nineteen mumble as if to himself, "Maybe it's just as well."

Don't Fail to Begin Robert Leslie Bellem's Series About

a News-Cameraman——Next Month!

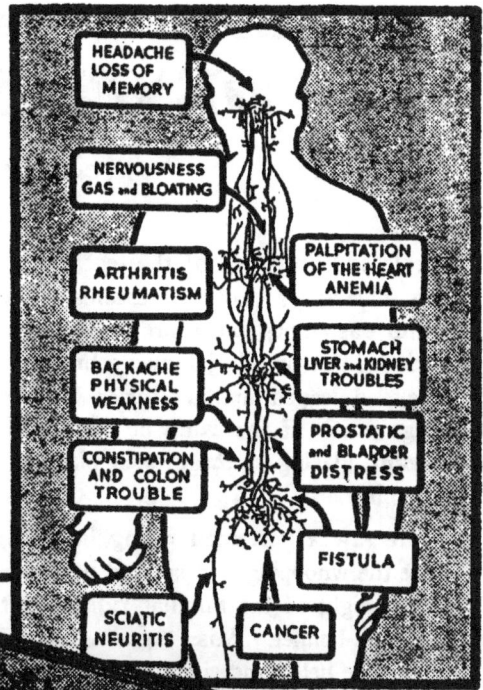
When answering advertisements please mention SPICY-ADVENTURE STORIES

DESERT BLOOD

[Continued from page 39]

girdle and burst out of the tent, ignoring Zulaykha's profane screams. The camp was empty, but spare horses were picketed nearby. He jammed a bridle on one and leaped up, bareback. On the ridge north of the camp he paused an instant, glaring at the broken plain below him.

He saw a horseman riding hard before the whooping Arabs. And he swore at the sight of the familiar riding-habit and sun-helmet. Miss Agusta Evans! What the hell! And riding as he'd never expected to see her ride.

She was making a wide circle, swinging back to the south again, and her horse was magnificent. She was drawing steadily away from all of them except Ali and he was barely holding his own.

CLANTON cut straight across the wide semi-circle, riding with a recklessness acquired by a boyhood on a Western ranch, before he went to sea. They were not far ahead of him as he rode to cut their path, when the woman's horse stumbled and threw her over its head. The girl staggered dizzily to her feet, just as Shaykh Ali swept down, yelling, sprang off and grabbed her in a way that showed plainly that he did not intend to postpone his favorite pastime.

Then Clanton heard him cry out fiercely and saw him dash his captive to the ground in a paroxysm of anger the white man could not understand. But Canton came sweeping in, and his yell was a challenge that brought Ali around, whipping out a pistol. They fired simultaneously. Clanton heard the whine of Ali's slug, and the Bedouin fell, with a bullet through his head.

Nearly half a mile back his followers yelled with panic, pulled up and scattered to cover, not recognizing their former prisoner at that distance, and fearing an attack in force.

Clanton leaped down and grabbed the girl, who was just getting on her feet. The helmet had fallen off, revealing a profusion of *black* hair!

"Aicha!"

She clung to him.

"Oh, my lover! When they rode away with you toward Ali's camp, I rode for Tebessa, to beg the French to come and aid you, though I feared they would arrive too late. But then Allah put the means of saving you in my hand!

"I knew Ali would ride forth with all his men if he sighted a white woman riding alone. So I showed myself in these garments to his sentry on the ridge, intending to draw them all away, outride them and double back to set you free before they could come up. But the horse stumbled."

"But where'd you get these clothes?" he asked.

"As I rode toward Tebessa, I met a white woman with spectacles on a donkey, and a boy guiding her whom I knew. Yussef, son of Hassan. So I gave him money, and we took her garments—"

"*What?*"

When answering advertisements please mention SPICY-ADVENTURE STORIES

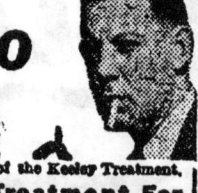

"Aye. Yussef helped me strip her. She made many lamentable cries, and wept with shame. Aye, she blushed from head to foot! She could have had *my* garments, but while I was preparing to change, Yussef put her upon her donkey and it ran away toward the city, she clinging to the saddle-horn, and—"

The rest was drowned in Clanton's roar of laughter as he was overcome by the thought of Miss Augusta Evans, on a runaway donkey, approaching the crowded streets of Tebessa, clad only in horn-rimmed spectacles. Aicha watched him, naively puzzled at his mirth, but glad that her new lord and master should be pleased with her. "And then Yussef ran away," she concluded, "and I rode on to Ali's camp, and all befell as you have seen."

Still laughing he caught his horse and hers, which were grazing nearby. He spanked her playfully as he lifted her into the saddle; she filled those provocative riding breeches even more deliciously than had Miss Evans.

"I'll have to sneak you into Tebessa and get you some more clothes before you're spotted with those duds on, and arrested for highway robbery! As soon as I've delivered those rifles to my Berber friends, I'm going to take you to sea with me. Ever been to sea, Aicha?"

She shook her head. He grinned with pleasureable anticipation.

"You'll like it, kid; wait till you see my ship's cabin!"